Dear Reader,

I was thrilled when I was asked to reprint *One Touch of Topaz*. It was the only one of my early books that had a limited release, so many of you who have been with me since those early days had not had a chance to read it. *One Touch of Topaz* was not only the book away as a special promotion to bring in new readers, but I spent longer writing it than I did many of the other love stories I was doing at the time. I loved the concept of Topaz—Samantha Keman—the freedom fighter who survived a revolution. As you know, I have a fondness for writing about strong, independent women who also have an element of vulnerability. I believe you'll find Fletcher Bronson a good match for her.

As for the plot, I tossed in passion, adventure, patriotism, and characters I cared about.

I hope you'll care about every one of those characters as much as I do.

Iris Johansen

Iris Johansen

Dear Reader,

I was very happy when Bantam decided to reprint *One Touch of Topaz*. It was the first of my early books that had a limited re-lease, so many of you who have been with me since those first years may not have had a chance to read it.

It was decided to give the book away as a special promotion to bring in new readers, but I spent longer writing it than I did many of the other love stories I was doing at the time. I loved the concept of Topaz—Samantha Barron—the freedom fighter who survived a revolution. As you know, I have a fondness for writing about strong, indepen-dent women who also have an element of vulnerability. I believe you'll find Fletch Bronson a good match for her.

As for the plot, I tossed in passion, adven-ture, patriotism, and characters I cared about—I hope you'll care about every one of those characters as much as I do.

Iris Johansen

Iris Johansen

PRAISE FOR IRIS JOHANSEN

"Iris Johansen knows how to win instant fans."
—Associated Press

"Iris Johansen is a powerful writer."
—*The Atlanta Journal-Constitution*

"[Iris Johansen is] one of the romance genre's finest
treasures." —*Romantic Times*

"A master among master storytellers." —*Affaire de Coeur*

"Johansen serves up a diverting romance and plot twists
worthy of a mystery novel." —*Publishers Weekly*

"[Iris] Johansen has . . . a magical quality."
—*Library Journal*

"[Johansen is] a consummate artist who wields her pen
with extraordinary power and grace." —*Rave Reviews*

"Iris Johansen is a bestselling author for the best reason—
she's a wonderful storyteller."
—Catherine Coulter

"Iris Johansen is incomparable." —Tami Hoag

BOOKS BY IRIS JOHANSEN

IRIS
JOHANSEN

~

One Touch
of Topaz

BANTAM BOOKS

One Touch of Topaz is a work of fiction. Names, characters,
places, and incidents are the products of the author's imagination
or are used fictitiously. Any resemblance to actual events, locales,
or persons, living or dead, is entirely coincidental.

2009 Bantam Books Mass Market Edition

Copyright © 1988 by Iris Johansen

All rights reserved.

Published in the United States by Bantam Books, an imprint of
The Random House Publishing Group, a division of
Random House, Inc., New York.

BANTAM BOOKS and the rooster colophon are registered
trademarks of Random House, Inc.

Originally published in mass market in the United States by
Bantam Books, an imprint of The Random House Publishing
Group, a division of Random House, Inc., in 1988.

ISBN 978-0-553-59310-5

Cover design: Julia Kushnirsky
Cover image: © Michael Goldman/Getty Images

Printed in the United States of America

www.bantamdell.com

2 4 6 8 9 7 5 3 1

One Touch
of Topaz

ONE

"The contact's code name is Topaz." Skip Brennen made a face. "Sounds like something from a spy novel, doesn't it? I feel like I should be wearing a trench coat and carrying a diplomat's attaché case."

"It's too damn hot to wear a trench coat." Fletcher Bronson slapped at a mosquito on his arm. "Hell, it's too hot to breathe on this forsaken island. I don't know what I'm doing here, anyway. Those thieving bastards will nationalize my refinery within the next six months no matter what they say now. I should have accepted my losses and not wasted my time coming to St. Pierre."

"Fat chance," Skip said with a drawl. "You don't like giving up anything that's yours. We both know you'd still have stormed down here if the junta had only threatened to confiscate one of the company trucks, much less a multimillion-dollar refinery."

"Maybe." Fletch gazed moodily at the emerald-green hills in the distance. The beautiful view from the balcony of this hotel suite that those megalomaniacs in the palace had given him was no doubt meant to soothe and calm. At the moment it did neither. "But I don't like Marxist juntas. I don't like thieves." He slapped at another mosquito. "And I don't like bugs."

Skip gave a soundless whistle as he leaned back in the rattan chair. Fletch's temper was evidently flaring at an all-time high. Not that it came as any surprise. Even on a good day Fletcher Bronson was a diamond in the rough who possessed an intimidating ruthlessness. On a particularly bad day he had seen that famous scowl cause corporate sharks and heads of state to quail and take a step back. And this was clearly a very bad day. It was no wonder the blustering and threats of the members of the junta had turned to deferential assurances when Fletch had confronted them that afternoon at the *palacio*. Fletcher Bronson was one of the foremost economic powers in this hemisphere, and he was known to let his displeasure be felt in no uncertain terms. This small refinery on St. Pierre may have represented only a minuscule percentage of Fletch's financial assets, but it *belonged* to him, and he never let anything that was his be taken from him without a fight.

"So what's the decision?" Skip asked quietly. "Do I fly you straight back to Damon's Reef, or do we make the trip into the hills and meet with Topaz."

"Topaz..." Fletch murmured, still looking at the hills in the distance. "I haven't decided. Could this be some kind of trap? Where did they contact you?"

"In the bar downstairs." Skip took a long pull on his whiskey and soda. "By a very luscious B-girl by the name of Maria Cruz, who seems to be exceptionally well informed regarding your business here. Ricardo Lazaro still appears to have a very strong network in the city in spite of his recent defeat by the junta."

"Is there any chance that this Lazaro will be able to launch another offensive?"

Skip shook his head regretfully. "The junta is firmly in power. Lazaro's men are scattered in the hills, running for their lives, and there's a rumor that Lazaro himself is wounded. It's a miracle they had the men and the weapons for this last raid on the Abbey."

"The Abbey?"

"The Abbey used to be a monastery. For the past six years it's been a prison for political prisoners"—Skip's lips tightened—"one they kept carefully hidden from the human-rights committee."

"Torture?"

"The works," Skip said succinctly. "You name it, they did it."

"Charming."

Skip nodded. "You've already discovered for yourself how charming this government can be."

Fletch's gaze returned to Skip's face. "And they want us to get these political prisoners they rescued off the island before the army rounds them up?"

Skip nodded again. "They have supporters in Barbados, and they've asked us to fly the prisoners there."

"How many are there?"

"Nine."

"Can the helicopter carry that many passengers?"

"Possibly. If we jettison everything except the bare essentials. It will be pretty close."

Fletch muttered a curse. "Dammit, this is none of our business. I don't want to become involved in these penny-ante Caribbean politics. Most of the time one side turns out to be as corrupt as the other."

Iris Johansen

"Then don't become involved. I only thought I should relay the message." Skip paused. "There's something else you should know. There are three children among those escaped prisoners."

"Children? What the hell were children doing in a prison?"

"Sometimes it's easier to make a prisoner talk if the torture is inflicted on members of the family."

The flesh tightened over the broad planes of Fletch's cheeks as his teeth clenched. He was silent for a moment, his green eyes growing more icy with every passing second. "I don't like that," he said softly. "No, I don't like that one little bit."

"I didn't think you would."

Fletch's hands tightened on the lacy black iron of the balustrade. "When is this pickup supposed to take place?"

"Tonight at ten o'clock. They gave me the coordinates." He shrugged. "They must be pretty desperate to run that risk. We could turn the information over to the junta in exchange for certain concessions."

Fletch looked at his wristwatch. "Three hours. We'd better get moving."

Skip straightened in his chair. "You're going to do it?"

Fletch smiled grimly. "You're damn right I'm going to do it. I don't like governments who use children as pawns in their vicious games. I'm going to enjoy the hell out of snatching them away from the junta. At least I'll get the satisfaction of taking something back from those thieving bastards. Can you have the helicopter serviced in time?"

"It's already serviced and ready to go," Skip said blandly. "I also stripped it down as much as I could without raising the suspicion of the maintainance men at the airport. What I couldn't get rid of, I unscrewed and loosened so that we can ditch it in the hills."

"You took a good deal for granted. I don't like being thought of as predictable, Skip."

Skip felt a chill run down his spine, unconsciously bracing himself as he met Fletch's gaze. Even after twelve years as his personal pilot and general jack-of-all-trades, Skip could still be made to feel uneasy by Fletch. He should have become accustomed to the man by this time, Skip thought. Wielding power had become second nature to Fletch, and he probably didn't even realize he was doing it.

Hell, most of the time Skip liked Bronson, and he always respected him. Fletch was honest, generous, fair, and, on rare occasions, displayed a wry sense of humor few were aware existed. He doubted if Fletch would ever let anyone get close enough to call him friend, but if he did, he would probably be a damn good one. "You like kids," he said simply. "I thought the odds were good you'd get mad enough to thumb your nose at our pals at the *palacio*." He grinned. "And why shouldn't I do a little mind reading myself? You have quite a few business rivals who claim you have occult powers."

Fletch's frown disappeared and a slow smile lit his face. "Why not, indeed? Sorry, Skip, this whole mess has put me on edge. I'll be glad to get off this damn island and back to civilization."

"No problem." Skip rose to his feet with loose-limbed grace and set his drink on the glass-topped table next to him. "If you can be at the front entrance of the hotel in fifteen minutes, I'll have a taxi waiting to take us to the airport. I'm going down to the bar and tell our luscious little B-girl we'll make the pickup so she can send word to Topaz."

"Have her tell him to have those prisoners ready to move out. I don't want to linger there any longer than necessary."

"Will do." Skip pulled the bill of his Cubs baseball cap down more firmly over his eyes and moved toward the French doors that led to the interior of the suite. "But it's not a 'him.' Topaz is a woman."

Where *were* they, blast it?

Samantha's gaze anxiously searched the night sky. There was moonlight tonight, which was both bad and good. It had made their journey from the hills to this glade easier, but it also made them easier to track. Ricardo was sure a patrol had spotted them.

The whir of a helicopter's rotors came faintly to her ears, and relief poured through her with dizzying force. Even after Maria had radioed the confirmation, Samantha had been afraid Bronson would back out. It had been a long shot that he would be willing to involve himself in their troubles, but they had to ask for his help; they'd had no choice.

"They've come?" Ricardo's voice made her jump.

She drew a deep, steadying breath and nodded. "I think so." Only a little longer. She only had to hold on a little longer, and Luz and the others would be on the helicopter. Lord, she was tired of being afraid.

Ricardo's hand was gentle as it clasped

her shoulder. "Take them to the helicopter as soon as it lands in the glade. I'm going to backtrack and see if I can spot the patrol."

"No, I'll go—" She stopped. He had already faded into the forest. She should have known better than to try to talk him out of anything, she thought wearily. He knew he shouldn't be walking on that leg any more than necessary. It might be only a flesh wound, but the bleeding had started again on the way from the caverns.

"Samantha?"

Luz was beside her, nervous and hesitant, as she had been since they had freed her from the Abbey.

Samantha nodded. "They're here, Luz."

Luz bit her lip, her gaze on the sky.

The helicopter was overhead now, slowly descending to the grassy clearing. The roar of the rotors shattered the stillness and brought a rain of fresh panic. Oh, dear God, was the patrol close enough to hear?

Luz slipped her hand into Samantha's and squeezed it gently. Samantha wasn't sure if the child was intending to give comfort or take it. Luz knew about fear, and she could probably sense Samantha's terror no matter how she tried to mask it.

The helicopter was now on the ground, the lights splaying brilliantly in a circle around it.

It was time to go.

Later Fletch would find it curious that the first thing he noticed about Samantha was her hair. Not that it wasn't lovely hair. The rich, vibrant chestnut mane shimmered under the lights; it was pulled away from her face and fastened in back with a plain tortoiseshell barrette. Then, as she stepped up to the bubble window to stand beside Skip at the pilot's controls, he saw her eyes and knew at once who she was and where she had gotten her code name. Her eyes were the color of topaz; not the pale, tawny gold of the Brazilian stone but a darker shade, closer to the amber tint of the jewel found in the wilds of Siberia. They dominated her thin, fine-boned face, blazing with vitality and strength. She was dressed in a worn khaki shirt, trousers that looked two sizes too big for her, and combat boots. Fletch experienced a violent and completely unexpected surge of resentment that had something to do with the obscene contrast the military garb made to the fragile grace of her body.

Then she smiled, and he forgot delicacy and remembered only warmth and radiance. "Thank you for coming," she said softly. "I'm Topaz." She shook her head wearily. "No, that's not right. It's hard to remember that everything's over and there's no reason to be cautious any longer. I'm Samantha Barton."

"Skip Brennen. This is Fletcher Bronson."

She nodded, scarcely giving Fletch a glance. "We have everyone ready to go." She waved to a huddled group on the edge of the glade, and they started toward the helicopter. "You two won't have to get out of the copter. There's a patrol on our heels, so we'll have to hurry. Ricardo and I will get them on board."

She walked quickly toward the rear of the helicopter and was sliding open the door by the time the first of their passengers reached her. Fletch felt a swift surge of pity as his gaze ran over the men, women, and children standing by the door. They looked as emaciated as the survivors of Auschwitz.

The adults boarded first, and then the children were lifted aboard. Finally there was only one gangly girl of twelve or thirteen with enormous dark eyes who clung to Samantha Barton like a shadow.

"You have to get on the copter now, Luz," Samantha said gently. "There's not much time."

The child shook her head.

"It's going to be fine. We have people who will take care of you and send you to a fine school."

The child only clung closer.

Suddenly a man limped to Samantha's

side, a frown marring the classic handsomeness of his face. "Samantha, for all that's holy, get her on board. That patrol will be here within ten minutes."

Fletch was abruptly jarred from his fascination with both Samantha Barton and the scene unfolding before him. He had been sitting back objectively viewing these people as if they were on a movie screen. It was completely out of character for him to stand on the sidelines without participating in the action. "Let's get going. I have no desire to spend any more time in this wonderful island paradise, and certainly not as the guest of the junta."

Samantha gave him an exasperated glance. "I'm trying. Luz is—" She suddenly fell to her knees, clasped the child's thin shoulders, and gazed into her face. "Luz, listen. You'll be all right. It was a terrible thing that happened to you, but it's over now. The hurt won't stay unless you let it. If you're strong, the pain will only make you stronger and more beautiful. I've told you this so many times before, and it's true, Luz. You don't need me. You don't need anyone. Go now." She smiled. "I can't leave until you take off, and you don't want them to catch me, do you?"

Luz shook her head and then hurled herself into Samantha's arms. Then she was gone, scrambling into the helicopter.

Samantha gave a sigh of relief. "That's better."

"Can we go now?" Skip asked.

Samantha nodded. "That's all. We can't thank you en—"

"No." The Adonis with the bandaged leg and the limp shook his head. "One more passenger." He smiled at Samantha, his white teeth flashing in his dark face. "Get on board, *querida*. This is the end for you." He turned toward the cockpit. "Can you make room for one more? She doesn't weigh much."

"Skip?" Fletch asked.

"She shouldn't weigh much more than one of the children. I think we can manage."

Samantha stood very still, gazing at the wounded man. "You were planning this all along, weren't you, Ricardo?"

He nodded. "Don't argue with me, Samantha." He suddenly looked unutterably weary. "It's over, and there's no way you can help us now. You know what they'll do to you if they catch you."

"I'm not arguing." She smiled faintly. "We don't have the time. But would it be too much to ask you to give me a good-bye hug?"

"Samantha..." Ricardo enfolded her in his arms. "Go with God. You know I—" He broke off. He stood quite still, swayed, and then slowly crumpled to the ground.

Samantha stood clutching a small hypodermic needle in her left hand. "Go with God, Ricardo," she whispered. "I'll miss you."

"What the hell!" Skip was staring in bewilderment at the man on the ground. "What did you do to him?"

"It's only a sedative. He'll wake up within

the hour." She was still staring down at the fallen man with glittering eyes. "I knew he would try to put me on the helicopter so I was prepared." She lifted her head. "Will you help me with him? We have to get him on the helicopter right away."

Skip shook his head. "We can't take him. He weighs too much."

"But I'm not going," she said desperately. "And Ricardo only weighs about one hundred and sixty pounds. That's not so much." She took a step closer to the glass-enclosed bubble of the cockpit. "Look, you've *got* to take him. He's Ricardo Lazaro, and it's only a matter of time before they catch him. You have to get him off the island."

"A hundred and sixty pounds..." Skip shook his head. "That's still too much weight."

A shock of fear shivered through Samantha. "Isn't there something else you can take out?"

"The copter's already stripped. I'm sorry, but you'll have to leave him."

"I can't." This was truly the end then, she thought numbly. The end for both her and Ricardo.

"Take him." The passenger door was opening and Fletch Bronson was stepping to the ground.

Skip immediately protested. "Fletch, we can't—"

"I'm staying. You won't have a problem with weight."

Fletch was coming around the front of the 'copter, and Samantha's eyes widened. She had been so tense and absorbed, she had been only marginally aware of Bronson as a shadowy figure in the passenger seat. There was nothing shadowy about the man coming toward her with swift, impatient strides. She had seen pictures of him in the newspaper when he had first arrived on St. Pierre four days ago, but they had failed to capture the presence of Fletcher Bronson. The man was a Titan. He stood at least six-five and was too large-boned to be considered slim, though there was no spare flesh on his body.

He was probably in his early forties; his auburn hair, closely barbered to suppress rebellious curls, was threaded with silver. The planes of his cheeks were broad, his rust-colored brows thick, bold slashes above those cool green eyes. No one, Samantha thought, would call him good-looking. Yet there was something fascinating about his bone structure, a subtle beauty in the well-defined curve of his lips that made one want to keep looking.

He picked up Ricardo as easily as he would a sleeping child, deposited him in the helicopter, and slid the door closed. Then he stepped back and grasped Samantha's elbow, carrying her with him away from the aircraft. "Now get out of here, Skip. Come back for us tomorrow night about this time. It should be safe by then."

"But what if—"

"Move!"

Skip sighed as he turned on the ignition and the propellers started whirring. "I'm

moving already." A moment later the helicopter rose sluggishly into the air.

Fletch immediately turned to Samantha.
"I gather we can't wait to bid them a lingering farewell?"

Samantha shook her head. "The soldiers
will be here any minute." She turned and set
off across the glade toward the shadowy
protection of the rain forest. "Come with
me."

"I intend to," Fletch said dryly. "I have no
intention of wandering around in these hills
by myself. Do you know a safe place to hide
out tonight and tomorrow?"

Samantha smiled back over her shoulder.
"Don't worry, I know a place. I'll take good
care of you."

She meant it, Fletch realized with shock. It
was absurd, of course. He hadn't needed
anyone to protect or care for him in more
years than he could remember, and he certainly had no confidence in Samantha's abil-
ity to do so, either. She looked as ethereal
as the moonlight. Too damn ethereal. He felt

an odd resentment as he saw how loosely her khaki trousers hung on her slim hips. "Since you're not even carrying a rifle, you'll forgive me if I find it difficult to believe you could overpower a patrol. Lazaro's forces must have been even more impoverished than I've heard if he couldn't afford to give his followers weapons."

"I don't like guns," she said simply. "Ricardo knew that and never suggested I use one. I was principally a courier and radio operator."

"How understanding of Lazaro."

"Ricardo is very understanding," she said earnestly. "And weapons won't help if the patrol catches up with us. We'd do better to avoid them. I know these hills, and I won't let you be caught."

"Thank you," he said, and for some reason he found the intended irony entirely missing from the words.

"It's I who should thank you," she said gravely, "for giving up your place to Ricardo. I owe you a great debt."

"You don't owe me anything," he said bluntly. "I never do anything I don't want to do. I just had too much sense to stand there arguing until the soldiers appeared and caught all of us."

A tiny smile tugged at the corner of her lips. "I see. Well, then I'm grateful that you're so sensible. It was a lucky break for Ricardo and me."

Her steps quickened as she entered the luxuriant, junglelike shrubbery of the rain forest.

Fletch pursed his lips in a soundless whistle as he looked around the cavern. "Well, I'll be damned. You obviously do all right for yourselves. As a hideout, this is on the grand scale."

"It is pretty, isn't it?" Samantha moved the lantern in her hand, playing the light over the walls of the cave on either side of the stony path they were traversing through the cavern. Stalactites, varying in shades from cream to peach-amber, hung like giant icicles from the ceiling far above them. "It's very safe, too, with that thick brush cover in front. We were lucky to find this place."

"How long have you used these caverns?"

"About two years." Her tone was somber. "When we first discovered it, things were much different. There were still more than five hundred of us. We had hope." She straightened her shoulders as if shrugging off a burden. "Well, that's in the past. When Ricardo finally realized four months ago that he wasn't going to be able to overthrow the junta, he disbanded his forces, telling his men to go home. Then there were only four of us left. Ricardo, me, Paco Ranalto, and Dr. Salazar. We managed a few last raids on the Abbey, but we all knew it was really the end. Ricardo sent Paco and the doctor away two days ago, but he still needed someone to help get the refugees off the island. He didn't argue with me when I told him I wouldn't leave him."

No, she wouldn't have left Lazaro, Fletch

thought with a pang that was strangely like the throb of a fresh wound. That last embrace they had shared had practically shouted of the love existing between them. "What would have happened if you'd been caught with him?"

"Nothing very pleasant." The lightness in her voice was obviously forced. "But I would have survived. I wasn't really important to them. The junta wanted Ricardo badly to make an example of him. You were his last chance to get off the island, but I knew he wouldn't take it."

"So you saw that he did. Where did you get the sedative and the hypodermic?"

"From Dr. Salazar. He brought Ricardo into the world and knew we had to save him. He loves him very much."

"As you do?"

She glanced over her shoulder, and her thin face was again illuminated by that incredibly radiant smile. "As I do."

Fletch experienced another twisting pain of an intensity that shocked him. Why should the woman's willingness to sacrifice her life for Lazaro matter? She was nothing to him. Granted, she possessed a rather ethereal beauty, but he had never been attracted to her type before. His mistress of the moment was dark, lush, and experienced enough to please even the most demanding voluptuary. This child would break in his hands.

"How old are you?" he asked abruptly.

She looked at him in surprise. "Twenty." Her brow wrinkled in a frown. "No, that's not right. I must be twenty-one. We never thought much about birthdays here."

Another emotion rained through him, this one more maddening and far more poignant. Tenderness. A child with no birthdays, a child who lived in a cave surrounded by violence and fear, a child alone...No! He *wouldn't* feel like this. This entire scene was completely unlike him, and so were his reactions to Samantha Barton. She had not been alone. She was Ricardo Lazaro's woman, a camp follower who had chosen her way of life. "How long have you been with Lazaro?"

"Six years."

That would have to make her about fifteen when she first bedded Lazaro. How could she have made any kind of voluntary choice at that age? Another emotion flashed through him, much stronger and now clearly recognizable as jealousy. The image of her coupling with Lazaro, lying beneath him, those slim fingers clutching his bare shoulders as he—

"How old are you?"

He was jerked back to the present. "Thirty-seven."

"I thought you were older."

Compared to that damn Adonis she was sleeping with, he was a Methuselah. "I'm old enough."

She laughed. "That was rude, wasn't it? It's not that you look old. As a matter of fact, you're sort of ageless. Like that Ayers rock in Australia, or maybe one of those Easter Island statues."

"Thank you."

She paid no attention to the irony of his words as she gazed at him thoughtfully. "No, that wasn't the reason I thought you were older. You've accomplished so much with your life in those thirty-seven years. I read all about you in the paper when you arrived on St. Pierre. Are you really a billionaire?"

"Yes."

"I bet you don't give yourself much time to spend all that money." She was still studying him, and he was reminded of the curiosity of a small child. "I think you're the kind of man who likes the battle more than the prize."

His lips curved with sudden humor. "It depends on the prize. I assure you I have quite sybaritic tastes on occasion. For instance, under normal circumstances I'd find your pretty cavern tolerable for all of thirty minutes."

"It grows on you." She laughed suddenly, her topaz eyes dancing as she gestured around her. "Like those stalactites. Lord knows, I've sometimes felt I was turning into one when we were forced to stay in here weeks at a time." She shot him an impish sidewise glance. "I'll try to get you out of here and on that helicopter before you truly turn to stone."

"Me? You're speaking in the singular. There's no reason why you can't come with me. There'll be plenty of room on the helicopter tomorrow night."

"I can't leave yet. Paco still has to be gotten off the island."

"You said Lazaro sent him to his home."

"It was the only solution at the time. Dr. Salazar will probably be safe in his village, but Paco was Ricardo's first lieutenant and someday someone will find out who he is and expose him to the junta."

"But my helicopter was supposedly your last chance of getting anyone off the island."

Her jaw set with determination. "I'll just have to find another way."

"And get yourself captured while you're

trying to rescue him?" He could hear the harshness in his own voice, but he didn't try to temper it. She intended to stay here alone; the realization filled him with a panic as unexplainable as the other emotions that had assaulted him since she had stepped into the pool of light at the helicopter. "What a stupid thing to do."

"Maybe." Her lips were trembling as she tried to smile. "But I have to do it." She quickly changed the subject. "I won't make you walk much farther. There's a place up ahead where you can make yourself comfortable. It's like a lovely, huge room. There are several areas similar to it in the caverns, but this is the largest." She hurried on ahead, her voice echoing back to him. "It gets awfully cold in here at night, but we have blankets and can build a small fire."

"Samantha, you can't stay..." His words trailed off. She wasn't listening and was walking so swiftly, he had to lengthen his stride to keep her in view.

He turned the corner and stopped in

amazement. The expanse before him *was* similar to the huge, high-ceilinged room to which she had compared it—providing that room had been located on another planet. It was a good fifty feet long, forty feet wide, and the stalactites hanging far above him gave the entire area the appearance of an alien landscape. A cave on the moon might have looked like this, he thought. It would possess the same sterile beauty, the same chilling magnificence.

"The pool over there is fed by a fresh spring that empties into a lake after it leaves the cavern." Samantha lit a large candle affixed to the stone wall by a crude black iron sconce. "It's ice-cold but adequate for bathing."

The signs of human habitation were sparse, a shortwave radio against the far wall, several khaki canvas backpacks, two battered metal trunks, a tin coffeepot and dishes stacked by a pile of beige army blankets. Small stones encircled the blackened ashes that was all that remained of a campfire, and wood was stacked in readiness beside it. She had lived here for two years, he realized. How would it feel to live in this soulless emptiness for that length of time?

"And these blankets are clean," she said earnestly. She took four of the beige blankets from the stack against the wall and hurried back to spread two of them, doubled over, on the hard stone floor before the ashes of the campfire. She then spread the other two blankets on the other side of the circle of stones against the cavern wall. "There. At least that's better than the ground. Are you hungry?"

"I could eat."

"We have bread and cheese." She hurried to one of the canvas bags and extracted a quarter of a loaf of bread and a bit of Swiss cheese wrapped in foil. She placed them both on the blanket and then straightened. "You can start on that. There are plenty of rations in another room of the cavern. I'll go get them."

"That's not necessary."

"It's no trouble." She flashed him another smile as she picked up the lantern. "Eat. I'll be back soon."

She walked quickly out of the room in the direction from which they had come, and he heard her footsteps echo and then fade away.

Loneliness. Fletch was suddenly conscious of a terrible aloneness as he stood there in the immensity of stone and space. Aloneness, silence, and an awareness of his own vitality, the blood running through his veins, his humanity in a place that seemed inhuman. Lord, he was growing imaginative, he thought in disgust. This was just a cave, Samantha Barton was merely a woman, and day after next he'd be done with both of them and back to his own life.

He crossed the room and dropped down on the blankets Samantha had spread for him. He had missed dinner, and his stomach was now reminding him of that omission. He reached for the bread and cheese and began to eat.

She had to face it, there was a possibility she would die before she managed to leave the island.

Samantha breathed in the warm night air, trying to fight down the fear that persisted in rising within her. She couldn't hide forever from the knowledge just because it made her sick with fear. She had been frightened before but never like this. Then it had been a shared fear with Ricardo and the others, an emotion she could deal with if she found something to laugh about or had someone to reach out and touch when the panic came. Now she was alone, and no one knew better than she how dangerous the next few months would be. Her chances of surviving were pitifully slim.

Unless she got on that helicopter the following night.

Why not? She wanted to *live,* dammit. It was like a wild hunger in her. There were so many things she wanted to do and see and feel. She had done nothing but run and hide for as long as she could remember. Didn't she deserve something?

But Paco deserved to live, too, and she couldn't desert him and go her way. Their friendship had been forged in the most enduring flames of all. Ricardo and Paco had shared their laughter and their meager rations, as well as the danger, since they had taken her from the Abbey six years ago. Even while fear and wild rebellion were clawing at her, she knew she couldn't change her decision. She had to stay on St. Pierre.

It was no good standing here daydreaming, she thought, suddenly impatient with herself. There were some roads a person was forced to travel, and this was one of them. She would just have to find a way to crush the cowardice that held her in its thrall. She checked her wristwatch. She had given Fletcher Bronson over an hour, and that should be enough time.

She picked up the lantern she had set on the ground beside the entrance of the cave and began to wend her way quickly toward the room where she had left him. Relief surged through her as she realized she wasn't yet alone. Tonight, at least, she would have this man, stranger though he was, for company. She would get him to talk to her, and that should help stave off her fear.

A tiny smile curved her lips as she thought how annoyed Fletcher Bronson would be to know she intended to use him as a distraction. She had the impression that he allowed no one to use him in any fashion whatever.

What an unusual man he had turned out to be. She was accustomed to tough men, but he was more than tough. His physical prowess was matched by a depth of inner strength she could only sense, and he protected himself with a wall of barbed sharpness that allowed no one near. He was blunt to the point of rudeness and evidently said exactly what he thought and no more. His bluntness had amused and intrigued rather than offended her, and for a moment she wondered why, before dismissing it as unimportant. No matter how difficult the man might be personally, he had come when they needed him, and for that reason alone she was desperately grateful.

She turned the corner and saw him sitting on the blankets, his arms looped around his knees. Every muscle of his big frame breathed impatience and pent-up tension, and she was suddenly aware of the power of his large body. The massive muscles of his thighs were outlined, rather than concealed, by the fabric of his jeans, and his brawny shoulders strained against the cream-colored shirt as if fighting to get free. The sleeves of his shirt were rolled up to the elbow revealing the strength of his forearms. Looking at him, she felt a strange tingling in her palms and the arches of her feet.

She tried to smile and found herself breathless. Stranger still. "I'm sorry I was so long. I was searching for the rations, but I'm afraid they weren't any good any longer, so I had to toss them out. Did you have enough?

Perhaps if there aren't any patrols around, we can find some fruit in the jungle tomorrow morning. Sometimes we can—"

"There's no more food?" Fletch's question cut through her words like a machete. "None?"

She shook her head, avoiding his gaze as she moved across the room to set the lantern on the ground beside the blankets. "But I can build a fire now and make coffee. Perhaps that will satisfy you. I'm really very sorry."

"Will you stop apologizing?" His voice was so harsh, her gaze snapped back to him. She inhaled sharply as she saw his face. A flush was mantling the broad line of his cheeks, and his eyes were blazing pale fire at her. "Dammit, you *lied* to me. Do you think I'm some kind of idiot that I can't read you? There was never any more food, was there?"

"There's no need to be angry," she said soothingly, taking an involuntary step back. She could feel the waves of power radiate from him, power that was now charged with rage. "It's not important. Tomorrow—"

"To hell with tomorrow." He was on his feet and moving toward her. "And I've every reason to be angry." He grasped her shoulders and shook her. "That was the last of your rations, wasn't it? You lied to me. You gave me that food and went away, knowing I wouldn't eat it if you sat there and didn't take a bite or—"

"I wasn't hungry," she said, interrupting, trying to stem the flow. They were so close, she could feel the furnacelike heat emanating from his body and the smell of clean soap and a woodsy aftershave. "I had something to eat this morning."

"What?" he fired at her.

She moistened her lips nervously. "Fruit, I think. Something."

His hands tightened on her shoulders. "You're not telling me the truth."

"All right. Maybe it was last night."

"Maybe," he repeated with soft menace.

"Or maybe not. When did you eat last, Samantha?"

She gave up. "Yesterday afternoon." Then, as she saw his face darken, she hurried on. "But I had all the melon I wanted then. It was only because the patrols showed up that I didn't eat after that. There were only enough rations for the prisoners in the cavern. They were in much worse shape than Ricardo and me, so we—"

"Gave them your food," he said grimly, finishing her sentence. "And was I in worse shape, too, that you felt compelled to give me your last bit of food? Look at me, I'm built like a bull, and if I miss a meal, it's because I forget or I'm too busy, not because there's no food to eat." His fingers spread on her shoulders, testing their fine-boned frailty. "And you...Dear Lord, you're skin and bones. Do you know how this makes me feel?"

"I didn't mean to make you feel guilty." Her voice was gentle. "I'm sorry."

"If you don't stop saying that, I'm going

to throttle you." His eyes were blazing down at her. "Why, dammit?"

She raised her head and looked him directly in the eyes. "You were my guest," she said with dignity. "It was only right that I offer you what I had."

A look of stunned disbelief spread over his face. "Your idea of hospitality is carried to the extreme. Where the hell is your common sense?"

"I guess I don't have any." She smiled faintly. "I'm pretty impulsive, and I often leap before I look." Her smile faded. "But I didn't do that this time. I always try to pay my debts. I can never adequately repay you for saving Ricardo and the others, but I have to do what I can."

"I don't take food from starving women."

She shook her head. "I'm not starving. I'm not even hungry. I'm very tough, you know. I've gone far longer with much less." She smiled again. "And once I've had a cup of coffee, I'll be fine."

He gazed down at her intently, his eyes

narrowed on her face. His big hands were still kneading her shoulders, but she wasn't sure he was aware that he was doing it. He appeared totally absorbed, as if he were trying to unravel a complex and very irritating problem.

But if he was unconscious of his hands on her body, she was certainly not. A strange languid heat seemed to be generated beneath his palms, and her flesh was taking on an excruciating sensitivity. She drew a deep breath. "Mr. Bronson?"

He didn't answer at first, and she thought he hadn't heard her. Then his hands slowly released her and he stepped back, his face expressionless. "Fletch." A grim smile indented the corners of his lips. "Since I've stolen your last crust of bread, I believe formality is ridiculous." He gestured to the pallet against the wall. "Sit down. I'll make the fire and the coffee."

"No, I—"

He halted her protest with an upraised

hand. "I'm doing it," he said curtly. "Sit down and rest, dammit."

She slowly sat down on the blanket. "Very well." She crossed her legs Indian-fashion, resting her palms on her knees. "And then will you talk to me? I may be alone here for a week or two until it's safe for me to leave and go after Paco." She tried to keep her voice light and cheerful. "This might be my last chance for conversation for a while."

He gazed at her again with that curious intensity, his expression enigmatic. "Yes." He leaned down and began to lay the wood for the fire. "We can talk."

TWO

"Your English is very good. You don't have even the hint of the accent your friend Lazaro has. Are you an American?"

"My English should be good." Samantha laughed with genuine amusement as she took another sip of coffee from the tin cup. "I was born in Dallas, Texas. I wasn't aware that St. Pierre existed until I was ten years old."

"Interesting." Fletch cradled his own cup in his hands, gazing at her over the crackling flames of the fire. "Would you care to tell me how an American happens to belong to a revolutionary band on an island in the Caribbean?"

"My father was a newspaper man. Not a very well-known one, but he was bilingual and fairly competent. After my mother died, we came down here to live and he got a job as a reporter on the island's leading newspaper. It seemed like a good idea to him at the time. St. Pierre was the island paradise he'd always dreamed about. I liked it here too. I made friends and learned the language." She looked down into the coffee in her cup. "When I was fifteen, the junta overthrew the government, and suddenly I didn't like it here any longer. Neither did my father. Unfortunately the junta didn't like either my father or his stories in the newspaper. They killed him."

The baldness of the statement was more poignant than a more emotional recital ever would have been. "You loved him?"

"Yes." She took another sip of coffee. "So I joined Ricardo in the hills, and I've been here ever since." She lifted her gaze to meet his own. "That's all. Now tell me about you. I'm sure your life is much more interesting than mine has been."

"I believe a good many people would give you an argument on that score. What do you want to know?"

"Everything." She smiled. "I'm very curious about you. I've never met a tycoon before. Do you have a family?"

"No."

"That's too bad. You probably need someone to spend your money. I bet you're too busy to do it yourself."

He went still. "Are you volunteering?"

"Who me?" She shook her head. "I'm going to be very busy here on St. Pierre. You'll have to find someone else for the job." She chuckled. "Besides, you need someone who knows all the brand names. I don't know a Rolex from a Dior."

His eyes twinkled. "I think you could tell the difference. One is a wristwatch, the other is a couturier."

"You see? I'd be hopeless." She rested her chin on her drawn-up knees and gazed into the fire. "This is nice, isn't it?"

"You're easily pleased."

"I guess I am. Sometimes it's enough just to be alive, with a fire to warm you and someone to talk to." She shivered. "I get scared sometimes. I'm not very good at being alone."

Yet she refused to give up and leave this hellhole of an island. Anger and frustration surged through him, sharpening his voice. "If you intend to stay here, you're going to have to grow accustomed to it."

She nodded. "I will. Do you mind being alone?"

"No, it's never made any difference to me. I've been alone most of my life."

"Then you must be very strong." She studied him intently. "I think you'd be a good person to lean on when things got rough. It's a pity you don't have a family. Don't you like children?"

"As a matter of fact, I do like them. I'd like very much to have one of my own." His lips twisted cynically. "Unfortunately, acquiring a child usually involves marriage or at least some form of permanent relationship. I've discovered I have neither the time nor the inclination for either."

"I see." She shook her head. "Too bad. Maybe you'll change your mind someday."

"It's not likely." His face became expressionless again. "I prefer to avoid complications, and a situation involving a permanent companion is definitely a complication to a man in my position. For one thing, I enjoy the hell out of my work, and I'm not about to let a woman interfere with it."

"The battle, not the prize," she said softly.

He grimaced. "Well, I'm no prize myself. I'm a hell of a lot better in the boardroom than on the social scene. I don't understand all the fancy subliminal footwork that goes on at cocktail parties. I believe in taking what I want and paying for it."

"The two concepts seem at odds."

"Not really." His gaze zeroed in on her face. "You took what you wanted tonight when you unloaded that hypodermic into Lazaro, and you paid the price when you stayed in his place. I believe our philosophies are basically very similar."

She thought about it. "Perhaps you're right, but you violated your philosophy tonight when you jumped out of the helicopter so that Ricardo could leave. You took nothing, but you still paid. How do you explain that? Impulse?"

He shook his head. "I'm seldom impulsive, though I rely heavily on my instincts at times."

"And your instincts told you there was something worth staying for on St. Pierre?" She shook her head, her eyes sad. "I wish it were true, but everything of value vanished when the junta took power. You're going to be disappointed."

"I don't think so," he said slowly. He met her eyes again across the fire. "Sometimes the prize doesn't become visible until you tear through the nonessentials. There may be something I want very much on St. Pierre."

She could see the flames of the fire in his green eyes, and she gazed at him in helpless fascination. Compelling power was always mesmerizing, and every line and plane of his face sang with power. Power and something else that robbed her of breath and made her oddly dizzy. With an effort she pulled her gaze away. "Well, you don't have long to find out," she said lightly. "Your helicopter will be back tomorrow night." She finished her coffee in two swallows and set the cup on the ground. "I think I'll get a breath of air. Would you care to come along? I'd like to show you something special."

"Why not? I don't have anything more pressing to do this evening." He rose to his feet and reached out to pull her up to stand beside him.

She smothered a little gasp and tried to keep her expression as composed as Fletch's.

It had been nothing, she told herself. That tiny jolt of arousal when he had touched her had to be three parts imagination and one part sexual chemistry. But her hand was still tingling, and she found she was trembling. She casually withdrew her hand and turned away. "Hand me that lantern, will you? We have to go through three passages to reach my window."

A window in a cave? Fletch wondered as he followed Samantha through the curving passages. Well, it would be no more bizarre than anything else he had encountered that night. The lantern light cast shadows before them on the walls of the cave and caught gleams of gold in Samantha's chestnut hair. Richness and fragility should not have existed side by side, but in Samantha they did. The golden olive of her skin, that shining hair, those impossibly beautiful eyes were all full of vibrance and color, yet she still appeared as evanescent as morning mist.

Her shoulders had felt as breakable as the Fabergé egg on his desk in his study at home. And he had wanted to keep touching her as he touched the Fabergé. He wanted to run his hands over her warmth and explore and test that fragility. The urge had been so strong, he'd had to force his hands to release her. What was the fascination she was beginning to hold for him? No, not beginning. The fascination had been there from that first moment at the helicopter. It was only in the last few minutes he had realized that something else had entered into the picture.

Desire. Aching hunger like nothing he had ever felt before, reaching out, imprisoning him with silken skeins. He had watched the firelight play on her thin face; the arch of her throat as she had thrown back her head to laugh; the quick, nervous grace of her slim hands; and he had wanted to come to her with an intensity that dominated his entire being. Come, take, possess, and hold... Even now he could feel the heat flood his loins as he looked at her. Dammit, he didn't want this. He liked to have control of his body as he did everything else in his life, and there was no control here. He was like a stallion after a mare, lost in a mindless haze of sexuality.

"It's right at the end of this passage," Samantha called back over her shoulder. "I promise you that it's worth the walk."

He wanted her. Why not take her? A sexual attraction of this strength was seldom one-way, and there had been a few moments back there by the fire when he had seen something flare up in her that had reflected his own hunger. She might have been Lazaro's woman, but she wanted him now.

He smiled grimly as he realized he had already mentally consigned her relationship with Lazaro to the past tense. Well, it *was* in the past, he decided with sudden recklessness. This damn island had taken something from him, and now he would take something from it. She had no business staying here risking death and imprisonment, anyway. He would take care of her, see that she was safe and lost that air of delicacy. He was rationalizing, he thought with disgust, giving himself excuses for taking what he wanted. Why couldn't he simply admit he would have done anything in his power to have her no matter what the circumstances?

Then he suddenly realized it was the blasted tenderness, the oddly poignant *caring* that was causing these inexplicable qualms of conscience.

"There it is." Samantha turned to him, her face glowing with delight. "Isn't it beautiful?"

His gaze followed her own and he nodded slowly. "It's wonderful."

Samantha's "window" was a natural opening in the cave that started two feet from the ground and stretched almost eight feet high and five feet wide. It overlooked a view of breathtaking beauty. Moonlight glittered on the dark waters of a large lake some thirty feet below and softened the wildness of the lush thicket of the surrounding hills with shadowy mystery.

Samantha was gazing at him in disappointment. "You don't like it?"

"I said it was wonderful."

"But do you *mean* it?" One slim hand reached out to grasp his arm. "I can't tell. Don't you ever change expressions? Tell me what you're thinking."

What he was thinking now was X-rated and would probably scare the hell out of her. Every muscle in his body had readied when she had touched him, and he could feel the throb of the pulse in his temple, fast and heavy.

Her hand released his arm as if she had touched something that had burned her, and she backed away with an uncertain laugh. "That was rude of me. I guess you have to cultivate a poker face when you do business with power figures." She lifted her chin. "But it's true. I'm sure it must be very frustrating to everyone in your circle when you give them only your stone face."

"I assure you I make certain everyone knows what I want," he said dryly. "No one's complained before."

"Maybe they know what you want," she said. "But not what you're thinking."

He studied her. "And knowing what I'm thinking is important to you?"

"Yes."

He was silent a moment, and then a smile lit his face, transforming its hardness with rare warmth. "Then I'll try to give you what you want. Ask and you shall receive."

Why hadn't she realized how attractive he was? she wondered as she gazed at him. He possessed none of Ricardo's startling good looks, yet when he smiled, it was as if he gave a rare gift of untold riches. She was suddenly breathless again, and the tingling between her thighs shocked her. What was happening to her? She wasn't stupid enough not to realize her response to him was intensifying with each passing moment, but she couldn't seem to stop the tide. She wasn't even sure she wanted to. As confusing and tumultuous as were the feelings Fletch generated within her, they at least made her feel

Iris Johansen

vibrantly alive and pushed back the fear waiting in the shadows.

Fletch was looking at her inquiringly. "Well?"

She stepped closer to the window and drew in the warm, sweetly scented air. "I won't take advantage of your offer at the moment, but I have another favor to ask when you leave St. Pierre. Will you make sure Luz is given the help she needs? The other refugees will be all right, I think. We have sympathizers in Barbados who will provide funds and help them resettle, but Luz—"

"Luz is the child you spoke to at the helicopter? She seemed very upset. What special help does she need?"

"She was gang-raped at the Abbey." Samantha continued to look down at the lake below. "It's a common interrogation method. They thought her father had information, and they used her to get it. Do you know what that can do to a child?"

"I can imagine." There was such savagery

- 58 -

in Fletch's voice that it forced Samantha's gaze back to his face. His eyes were glinting with icy fury in the lantern light.

"My God," he asked, "what kind of monsters run that place?"

She was silent.

"They killed your father," he said harshly. "You must want to murder every one of them."

"I did at first."

"Not now?"

She shook her head wearily. "Hatred can eat at you until there's nothing left, until you become the thing you hate. I try not to hate anyone now. It's better just to try to change the bad to good and help bandage the wounds."

"I'm sure that's very laudable, but I'm afraid I couldn't be as philosophical in your place. I'd enjoy too much inflicting a few wounds myself."

She could see that he'd enjoy it. The savagery in his face shocked her.

He noted her reaction and smiled mirthlessly. "You said you wanted to know what I was thinking. You should have stated a few reservations if you didn't want the raw product. My thoughts are sometimes not as pleasant and civilized as you might like."

"I'd rather know the truth," she said shakily. "You know you're actually more of a warrior than Ricardo. I often thought it strange that he should spearhead the revolution when he's far more suited for almost anything else."

"I suppose he has the soul of a poet?" Fletch asked caustically.

"Close."

Fletch frowned. "Well, I don't want to talk about your dashing young poet. I don't believe you'd like my thoughts on the subject."

"But you'd like Ricardo," she protested. "He's a fine—"

He touched her. The tips of his fingers rested on the pulse beating beneath her chin. It was a gossamer-light touch, but it sent heat rocketing through her and made her forget what she had been going to say. She moistened her lips with her tongue. "What are you doing?"

"Touching you." His fingertips trailed lightly to the hollow of her throat. Her pulse leapt crazily under the pads of his fingers.

"Why?"

"Because I want to." He held her eyes and a faint smile curved his lips. "And because I wanted to stop you from talking about Lazaro. I don't want to hear you even speak his name. He's out of the picture."

"No, he—"

His fingers moved quickly to her lips, and the words froze before they were spoken. Her lips were throbbing, growing pliant, swollen, as he touched them. His index finger slowly traced the outline of her lower lip to one corner and then back again. "Forget him," he said softly. "You know I can please you. The sparks have been flying between us since the moment we met in the glade tonight. I felt them. You felt them." He smiled that rare smile again. "I think we're both burning, aren't we, Samantha?"

"Yes." She could barely get the words past the dryness in her throat. Her breasts were rising and falling as she tried to force air into her constricted lungs. "I guess we are."

He took a step nearer, and his hands cupped her face in his palms. "I like the feel of you." His thumbs splayed out, savoring the textures of the planes of her cheeks. "You're light, almost weightless, yet there's a strength..." His head lowered slowly. "But not too much strength. It's very erotic for a man to know he has the power either to break or treasure something infinitely fragile." His mouth brushed back and forth over her lips, each movement a kiss. "I like that power, Samantha, but I don't think I could ever bear to break you."

His lips wooed with delicate sweetness, taking, giving, with a skillfull sensuality that made a moan rise from deep in her throat as pleasure cascaded through her in golden ripples of sensation. He lifted his head, and she could see a tiny muscle jerk on his cheek. "No, I could never hurt you." His tongue licked gently at her lower lip. "Open, love. I want to taste you."

Her lips parted and the magic began again, a deeper and more intimate magic. Her hands reached out blindly to clutch his shoulders. He was so big, there was so much power, so much beauty...

His heart was pounding against her breast, and his mouth was becoming hotter, more demanding. His teeth caught her lower lip and nipped teasingly. The tiny, elemental pain sent a shiver of hunger through her. He buried his face in the hair at her temple, his arms going around her to press her into the hollow of his hips. Arousal. Stark, bold hunger. "Let's get back to the blankets," he said thickly. "I probably wouldn't notice if I were lying on a bed of nails, but these rocks might mark you." He moved her yearningly against him. "And I don't want anything to mark you but me."

She was trembling. Pleasure. He could give her pleasure and beauty, and she would forget terror and loneliness. She had never wanted anything in her life as much as she wanted Fletcher Bronson at this moment. So fast. How had this happened? Why this man when no other had aroused this wild wanting within her?

"Samantha?" Fletch's voice was a soft demand.

She moved closer, and he gave a satisfied chuckle. "You had me scared. You want me?"

Oh, yes, she wanted him. She was aching, throbbing, with that hunger. "I want you."

"Good. Let's get the hell back—" He broke off. She was stepping back, pulling away from him. He stiffened, his eyes narrowed on her face. "What's wrong?"

"I'm sorry." She was still backing away, shaking her head, her eyes glittering in the lantern light. "I didn't mean ... I don't think ..."

"Are you saying no?" His voice was dangerously soft.

"I think it would be ... it's for all the wrong reasons."

Fletch cursed beneath his breath. "Reason has nothing to do with it. You *want* me, dammit. And I want you."

Her feet felt weighted, her whole body sluggish. She didn't want to do this, she thought wildly; all she wanted was to go back into his arms and press herself against his big muscular body and let him—No, it wasn't right. It wasn't fair to him, and it might not be fair to herself, either. She was too shaken to think right now. She drew herself up straight, trying to still the trembling of her body. "I didn't mean to be a tease," she said with dignity. "I'm not myself tonight, and you caught me off guard. I hope you'll forgive me."

He took a half step forward. "The hell I—"

He stopped, fighting for control. "Dammit, I'm *hurting*."

"I know." Her topaz eyes were shimmering with tears. "I'm so sorry."

He gazed at her, and then suddenly his lips curved in a rueful smile. "Not nearly as sorry as I am."

She breathed a sigh of relief. "You're not angry?"

"I'm not feeling very kindly toward you at the moment, but anger doesn't enter into it. I can't afford it."

That was a strange thing to say, she thought in bewilderment.

He leaned down and picked up the lantern and handed it to her. "Let's get back. Lead the way."

"Thank you for being so understanding," she said haltingly as she started down the passageway.

"I don't understand," he murmured behind her. "But I have every intention of understanding everything about you. Soon."

She could feel his gaze on her as she led

them through the caverns, and she found it acutely disconcerting. He wanted her. He was looking at her buttocks and her thighs and imagining his hands on her. She knew it, and the knowledge was bringing a warm, liquid weakness to her every muscle.

She was relieved when they finally reached the central room. She set the lantern down by the campfire. "It's beginning to get cool, isn't it? There are some more blankets. Shall I get you a few?"

"I won't need them." He dropped down on the pallet farthest from the fire. "I can't imagine being cold at the moment."

Samantha felt the color sting her cheeks as she sat down in her previous place across the fire. "Good night."

"I doubt it," he said dryly as he settled his big bulk on the pallet. He turned to face her, his head resting on his arm. "It won't be a good night for either of us." He paused. "Unless you change your mind."

She shook her head emphatically.

"The offer remains open." His gaze met

her own across the fire. "You want me, you know you do." His deep voice was all-coaxing male persuasion. "You don't have to be alone over there. All you have to do is come and lie beside me and I'll give you what you need. What we both need."

The temptation was almost irresistible. Even in repose Fletch's brawny body radiated power and virility. She remembered how warm and hard he had been as she had pressed against him, how safe and secure she had felt leaning on his strength. Sensuality or security? Which was her motivation? she wondered desperately. Perhaps it was both. Oh, she just didn't know. The only certain thing was that she was too bewildered to make a decision involving a man like Fletch Bronson.

"No." Her voice was almost inaudible.

"Think about it." He smiled. "I'll be here for you." It was a promise.

She leaned back against the wall and closed her eyes. She could feel his gaze on her again, and it was impossible to force her muscles to relax. He was lying there, wanting her, waiting. She could feel her heart start to pound harder, and she was excruciatingly aware of everything around her: the crackle and hiss of the logs on the fire; the liquid gurgle of the spring; the light, steady breathing of the man across the fire.

Fletch. Waiting.

THREE

She was dreaming again.

Samantha realized on some remote level that she was dreaming, but it made no difference, because the terror was real, even if the cause of it was not.

And the scene in the dream was always the same: the wide black mustache on the face of the general in the portrait on the crumbling stucco wall; the four officers sitting at the long table, their expressions all identical; the broken flagstones beneath her feet as she walked slowly toward them.

And Papa sitting a little apart from the others, gazing at her with an agonized expression, his lips drawn back from his teeth as if in pain.

Papa. No, don't—*Papa*!

She came away from the wall, her eyelids flying open. Her heart was beating as if it might burst from her breast, and great shudders were racking her body. It was over, she assured herself frantically. It was all in the past. She was not at the Abbey but here in the caverns. Safe. Fletcher Bronson was only a few yards away. What had happened was in the past.

But it could happen again.

If she stayed here, it could happen again. She could be captured and taken to that place. Her heart was racing so fast, she felt sick.

She *had* to stay. She mustn't be such a coward. Perhaps it would be better after Fletch left the island and no longer offered such temptation. A wrenching pain swept through her. He would leave and she would be left alone. She might die here, never knowing, never experiencing so many wonderful things. She might be taken to the Abbey and—

No! With wild immediacy she rejected her vision of the future. She might have to stay, but she would not be cheated. She had a right to some joy.

"Are you all right?" Fletcher Bronson gazed intently at her.

She drew a deep, quivering breath. "Yes." She moistened her lower lip with her tongue. "I'm fine." She began to quickly unlace the army boot on her left foot. She pulled it off and then began unlacing the right boot. "I had a bad dream." She tossed the other boot aside and stripped off her socks.

"Does that happen often?"

"I don't want to talk about it if you don't mind." She rose to her feet and began unbuttoning her khaki shirt with swift, nervous fingers. "It's over now. Do you want me to undress completely, or do you prefer to do some of it yourself? I understand many men—"

"I beg your pardon?" He stiffened to total immobility, his gaze on her fingers on the buttons. "I seem to be behind the times. Do I take it you've changed your mind?"

She nodded jerkily. "If you still want to do it." She stripped the shirt off and dropped it on the pallet behind her.

Something hot flickered in the depths of his cool green eyes. "Oh, I still want to do it. At the moment I can't imagine anything I want more." His gaze dropped to her small, uptilted breasts, naked now in the firelight. "You don't wear a bra. I couldn't tell in that oversize shirt."

She could feel the color heating her cheeks. He was so casual, as if she had undressed for him a thousand times before. "I don't need one, I'm not very big."

"I can see that. I'm going to be able to hold your breasts in the palms of my hands. I'll like that." He sat up. "Will you come here, Samantha? I want to touch you."

She hesitated, then crossed the few paces separating them and dropped to her knees beside him. For the first time she looked directly into his eyes. She inhaled sharply, a tiny thrill of excitement running through her. She had been mistaken. Fletch was not at all casual. She swallowed to ease the tightness in her throat. "You're not touching me."

He smiled. "I'm quite aware of the fact. I want to take my time. You're special, Samantha." He unclasped her tortoiseshell barrette and tossed it on the ground. "Very special."

"I'm skinny."

He nodded. "You're too thin. We'll have to do something about that. I feel as if you'll shatter if I put even one finger on you."

"Oh, no, I'm really very tough. I get lots of exercise."

His lips tightened. "Running through these hills dodging patrols, no doubt." His fingers threaded through her hair, and the slight tugging sent a frisson of hot delight down her spine. His hands suddenly tightened on her hair, and he pulled her head back to look into her eyes. "We'll do something about that too."

She scarcely heard him. He was close enough for her to feel the heat of his big body and a faint musky fragrance that was wildly exciting. She began to unbutton his shirt. "Do you mind? I want to see you."

"I'm not very pretty. Not like your Adonis, Lazaro." He pulled away from her and rose to his feet. "I'll do it." He stripped quickly and efficiently and stood before her, still scowling. "I told you I was no Adonis."

Not Adonis. There was nothing slim or elegant about him. Fletch was all bulging muscle and power, tree-trunk calves and thighs, tight buttocks, and flat stomach. The thick auburn hair roughening his chest was gilded with silver, and he looked fully mature, overpoweringly male. Not Adonis but perhaps Vulcan or Hercules.

Samantha gazed at him in fascination, experiencing a primitive stirring within her.

His enormous strength and virility were magnetic. "I like the way you look." She stared at his broad shoulders. "You're very big, aren't you?"

His frown deepened with anxiety. "I won't hurt you." He dropped to his knees, one hand cupping her breast in his palm. "I know I'm built like a mountain, but I'll be careful. You're so damn little." His eyes narrowed, and a flicker of relief replaced the anxiety on his face. "Your heart is beating double time. Maybe you don't care.... Does it excite you to know how different we are?" He plucked teasingly at her nipple. "It excites me." One hand began unfastening her belt as the other gently opened and closed on her breast. "I like to think how tight you are. How you'll squeeze me." His finger circled her nipple.

The tingling between her thighs appeared to be spreading, throbbing through every nerve in her body.

"You'll sheath me tightly. Like this." His

hand gripped her breast. "But I won't release you, like this." His hand released its pressure. "I'll keep going, moving until I—"

She didn't realize she had made a hoarse sound deep in her throat, but he heard it. He stopped, and his smile held a touch of savagery. "You want me? Now?"

She nodded. "Please," she whispered.

His chuckle held surprise as well as sudden tenderness. "What a polite little girl you are. It's I who should say 'please.' " He rose to his feet and reached down to pull her up. "Please, will you get rid of the rest of these monstrous clothes?" He was getting rid of them himself, even as he spoke. He kicked the garments aside and smiled down at her. "Please, may I pet you?" His hand cupped between her thighs, gently massaging her womanhood.

Her eyes widened in shock as impossible sensations convulsed her. Her hands grabbed wildly at his shoulders. "Fletch—"

"Shh, I haven't remembered to be this polite in a long time. I believe I'm enjoying it."

His fingers insinuated, stroked. "Please, may I pleasure you this way, Samantha?" His eyes studied her face. "And it *is* pleasure, isn't it?"

"Yes," she murmured, her eyes closed. "Wonderful."

"So are you," he said softly. "Wonderfully tight. Wonderfully ready for me. Open your eyes, Samantha."

She opened heavy lids, gazing at him languorously.

"That's what I wanted to see," he whispered. "I want to know you're wanting me." He drew her back down on the blanket. "I want to know you're mine." He gently pushed her back and came over her, his eyes blazing down at her. "And you are, aren't you?"

There was something wrong, she realized vaguely. There was a hardness in the demand that was at odds with the pleasure he was giving her. "I don't think—" She broke off as his fingers began the magic he had so recently abandoned. She bit her lower lip to keep from screaming, as wave after wave of desire engulfed her, drowned her. "Fletch, I can't..."

"I can't, either." He gazed down at her, his nostrils flaring, his eyes glittering wildly in the firelight. "I wanted to wait, but I'm going insane." His lips pressed hard against her own, his tongue driving, plunging wildly. "Will you take me, Samantha? Now?" His teeth were clenched, his face drawn as if in pain. "Please?"

That last entreaty was not in the same half-mocking tone he had used previously. It was gasped with a desperation that stirred a strange maternal tenderness within her. Her hand reached up to tangle in his thick curls. "Yes," she whispered lovingly. "Now, Fletch."

His lips covered her own as he entered her slowly, carefully. She could feel the tension in his every muscle as he tried to hold himself back from her. Fullness...She closed her eyes, savoring the deliciousness of the sensation. Yet it was not quite enough. She moved, trying to tempt him to give more.

"No, be still. I'm trying to . . ."

She knew he was only trying to be careful, but the deliberateness of his movements was driving her mad. She moved against him, fighting to take what he would not give her.

"Samantha, please, I can't stand—" Suddenly he groaned and plunged deep.

His mouth on hers smothered her single involuntary cry. Lightning-quick pain. Then, like lightning, it was gone. Now there was only fullness, beauty, a pleasure so intense that her head was spinning.

"Open your eyes." His voice was low, stunned.

Her eyelids opened, and she gazed up at him dreamily. His expression revealed even more than his voice how stunned he was, she realized hazily. Well, she was feeling pretty stunned herself, pleasure-struck and entirely bemused. "Wonderful," she murmured.

"How badly have I hurt you?" His voice

was harsh. "I didn't mean to hurt you. Why the hell—"

She lifted her head and stopped the words with her lips. "No. Wonderful. It's all wonderful." She clenched herself around him. "Go on."

A shudder ran through his body, and a low groan broke from him. "Samantha, I can't do this. I don't want to hurt you again."

"I don't care," she said fiercely. "I can't bear this. I want—" She broke off because the words were no longer necessary. He was giving her what she wanted. Thrusting, plunging, moving her body so she was bound still closer to him. Deep. Deeper.

Wild pleasure, hot hunger—she couldn't tell one from the other. They were both intertwined, bound as their bodies were bound, taking and giving.

Her hands tightened in Fletch's hair, her head thrashing from side to side as she drowned in a searing ravishment of the senses. Her lips parted as she tried to force air into her lungs.

"Beautiful." Fletch's voice was hoarse, jerky. "Lord, you feel beautiful. It's like nothing—It's too good, love. I can't hold on. Please." He leaned forward to kiss her. "Please try."

What was he talking about? Then she knew, as he drove with a force and wildness that carried her to the heights of rapturous sensation. To the heights and beyond.

She couldn't move. If she were not still bound to him, she was sure she would drift away and be lost somewhere in a sea of starlit darkness. But she *was* bound to him, she realized contentedly. She could hear the harshness of his breathing above her and feel the solid strength of his thighs on either side of her. His scent surrounded her, and she knew she would be able to recognize his musky male fragrance for the rest of her life.

She would open her eyes soon, she decided, because she wanted to look at Fletch's face. He had looked so beautiful in his need and vulnerability when he had pleaded with her to release him. She slowly forced her lids to open and recieved a shock. Fletch's face was no longer either vulnerable or pleading, but definitely grim. "Is something wrong?"

"What could possibly be wrong?" he said caustically as he moved off her. "Everything's absolutely wonderful!"

She thought she understood then. "You didn't enjoy yourself? I'm sorry I wasn't experienced enough to make it pleasant for you."

"Pleasant for *me*?" He drew a deep breath. "Just don't say another word for a little while. Okay?" He stood up and crossed to the pile of blankets against the far wall and brought one back to her. "Sit up."

She felt too languid and content to move, but she decided she'd better obey him. He seemed terribly upset for some reason, and she didn't want the moment spoiled by conflict.

She sat up and was immediately enveloped in the blanket. He tucked the blanket around her, carefully pulling her hair from beneath its confines and arranging the chestnut tresses down her back. Strange. Though she could sense the anger in him, every action was performed with the most exquisite tenderness. He clasped her hand onto the opening at the front of the blanket, moved back a few steps, and sat down.

He was truly a magnificent specimen, she thought dreamily, her gaze running over him in the firelight. All bronze power and rippling muscle. Why had she ever thought he wasn't handsome? Just looking at him now sent a shiver of remembered sexuality through her.

"Now I have some questions to ask you."

She smiled mischievously. "You told me not to talk."

His eyes narrowed on her face. "You seem in very good humor."

"I am. I feel marvelous. Perhaps it will be better for you next time."

"I think that's what I'm supposed to say

to you," he commented dryly. "I take it your first experience was not a disappointment?"

She shook her head. "It was wonderful. Thank you." She covered a yawn with her hand. "But I'm suddenly awfully sleepy. Does it usually have this effect?"

"Sometimes." He brought up his knees and looped his arms loosely around them. "But I'm afraid you'll have to bite the bullet until I get a few answers."

"You want to know why I was a virgin?" She shrugged. "I've been busy helping to fight a war since I was fifteen. I guess I never met anyone I wanted to make love with."

"Lazaro?"

"Ricardo and I grew up together. He's my friend." She yawned again. "Can I go to sleep now?"

"Not yet." His entire body took on a leashed tension. "One more question. Why?"

"What do you mean?"

"Why me?" His linked fingers tightened until his knuckles showed white. "First you say no, and then a complete turnaround. It was too damn sudden."

Her brow wrinkled in a frown. "You didn't seem to mind at the time."

"I was hurting so much that I didn't give a damn what your reasons were, as long as you let me have you."

"Then why should you care now?"

"Because you were a virgin, dammit," he shouted. "Whatever motivated you must have been pretty damn strong, and I don't flatter myself that the magnificence of my body was the draw."

She could tell him that if she'd been aware just how magnificent his body really was, it would have been, as it was now, an irresistible lure. "I did want you," she said evasively.

"Maybe, but that wasn't all. Why?"

She realized he wasn't going to give up; he would keep battering at her until she surrendered. She sighed. "I was afraid."

He stiffened as if she had struck him.

"Of me? My Lord, I wouldn't have forced you."

"No, not *of* you," she said quickly. "I knew you wouldn't hurt me. It was other things."

"What things?"

"I don't know." She shook her head wearily. "Death, the patrols, dying before I'd ever really lived." She looked down into the heart of the fire. "Then I had a dream..."

"What about?"

"It's not important." She lifted her gaze to meet his. "I suppose I used you. You have a right to be angry with me."

"Yes, I do, but not for the reason you seem to think. I can stand being used." His lips curved cynically. "I've been used any number of times. I know I'm no Casanova, and as long as the bargain is mutually beneficial, I have no objection to women taking what they want from me. But you did something different, you made me feel—" He stopped, searching for words. "I feel like

Attila the Hun! I'm healthy and strong, and the first thing you did was to fool me into eating your food and making you go hungry. And then you let me make love to you without telling me you were a virgin. I was so damn eager, I was clumsy as hell and probably hurt—"

"You didn't hurt me," she said, interrupting quickly.

"The hell I didn't. I must have—"

"No, really, it was wonderful. I enjoyed every minute of it. I'm only sorry you didn't find it pleasurable." She frowned worriedly. "I feel terribly guilty about that."

He was clearly exasperated. "*You* feel guilty? How do you think I'm reacting? I feel like a child molester."

"I'm not a child, and if anything, I'm the one who molested you."

"Do you realize how ridiculous that sounds?" It was evident she didn't, for she was gazing at him with the puzzlement of a child.

"It's not ridiculous at all. I thought I was

being exceptionally aggressive. Maybe not very skilled, but you have to admit I was enthusiastic. Would you like to do it again? If you'll help me, I'll try to please you more this time."

He wanted her. His body was hardening at just the thought of entering her again. Why the hell not? He could be very careful with her this time. She was willing, and he had never before been shy about taking what he wanted from a woman. Yet now he was experiencing a hesitation that was incomprehensible to him. "You said you were sleepy."

"I think you could wake me up." Her lips trembled as she smiled at him. "And I'd like you to hold me again. I felt so safe."

Safe. It was fear that had driven her to him before, and she was still afraid now, he realized. There might be desire mixed with that fear, but it wasn't the paramount emotion at the moment. She was bargaining something she thought he wanted for a fleeting moment of forgetfulness and security.

Though she didn't realize it, she was using him again, and he found he was feeling no resentment, only aching sympathy.

He rose to his feet in one lithe movement and crossed the few paces between them. He dropped down beside her, gathering her into his arms, blanket and all. He settled her against him, her cheek in the hollow of his shoulder. "Go to sleep," he said gruffly.

"You don't want me?" She cuddled close, her hair splaying out over his bare shoulder in a silken cloud.

"No," he lied. "Not now."

"Well, if you're sure..." Her eyes closed, and she turned boneless in his arms. "I am a little tired."

Tired? She was nearly asleep, he thought ruefully. "I'm sure." His arms tightened around her. "We'll talk in the morning. Go to sleep now."

"All right. Thank you." Her breathing was steadying, deepening. "It's very nice of..." She was asleep.

She was weightless in his embrace, and

her long lashes feathered her cheeks, accenting her delicate bone structure and the thinness of her face. He felt a wave of overpowering tenderness and possessiveness. His lips lowered slowly to brush against her temple as he tried to settle himself for the night. The ground was stony, and the ache in his groin reminded him that he still wanted this child-woman in his arms.

Lord, he hoped this attack of uncharacteristic gallantry would pass into oblivion as quickly as it had come. He had an idea it was going to be the cause of a damnably uncomfortable night.

FOUR

THE RICH AROMA of freshly brewed coffee drifted to Samantha, piercing the last lingering mists of sleep.

She opened her eyes.

"It's about time you decided to wake up." Fletch was pouring steaming coffee into a cup a few yards away. "I had no idea ladies of the guerrilla persuasion were so slothful. It's almost noon."

"I was tired." Sudden color flooded her cheeks as she remembered the reason she had been so exhausted that she had slept without stirring for all these hours. She scrambled to a sitting position, clutching the blanket around her. "Good morning. Did you sleep well?"

"Not very." He put the coffeepot on one of the stones edging the fire and rose to his feet. "You wriggle. It's disconcerting." He crossed the few yards separating them and knelt beside her, offering her the cup. "Drink this. It will wake you up. We've got to get you some proper nourishment, though."

"Thank you." She took the cup and sipped the hot liquid gingerly, gazing at him over the rim. He looked robust, vigorous, burning with restless energy. He wore his jeans and cream-colored shirt, but his hair was now damp and twisting in tight, rebellious curls, and she caught the fragrance of soap. "Your hair is wet. Have you been in the spring?"

He made a face. "That bucket of ice? No way. I told you I had the tastes of a sybarite. I borrowed your soap and a towel and went down to that lake you showed me from your window last night."

Her hand tightened on the cup. "You shouldn't have done that. What if the patrol had seen you?"

"The patrol didn't see me. I'm not a complete fool, Samantha. I chose a spot that was relatively screened from view." He reached out and pushed a stray chestnut lock behind her ear. "And it wasn't complete self-indulgence. I might have tried your ice bath if I hadn't had to leave the cave for another reason, anyway."

"What reason?"

"Food." He smiled grimly. "I wasn't about to let you go without eating any longer than necessary." He gestured to a bucket to the left of the fire. "Lord knows, it's not much. Just some berries and melons. I was afraid to run the risk of rigging a trap to capture any game with the patrols around."

"Could you have done that?" she asked in surprise. "Are you a hunter?"

"Not anymore." A shadow flitted across his face. "Not for a long time now."

"You don't like hunting?"

"I never liked it. It was something that had to be done." He abruptly rose to his feet and turned away. "I was in the special forces in 'Nam."

"Oh." She didn't know what to say. He seemed to be charged with explosive tension. She took a sip of coffee. "The newspaper article I read didn't mention that you fought in Vietnam."

"It wasn't fighting, it was—" He broke off, reached for the coffeepot, and poured himself a cup of coffee. "You may think I have the instincts of a warrior, but I assure you I had no liking for that kind of warfare. Now I do my battling in ways that don't involve bloodbaths for women and children." He looked down at his cup. "What did your newspaper article tell you about me?"

"Not much, really. That you have interests in oil, shipping, and computers." She smiled. "That you own an island in the

Carribbean called Damon's Reef, a château in France on the outskirts of Paris, a fabulous mansion on one of the islands off the Oregon coast. It all sounds very glamorous."

"Nothing else?"

She avoided his gaze as she took another sip of coffee. "Well, it did mention Monette Santore, the actress. Is she as beautiful as the article said?"

"She's not beautiful at all. She has a certain earthy appeal and the elegance and gloss that most Frenchwomen seem to be born with."

"She sounds fascinating. Has she been with you a long time?"

"She's not *with* me at all," he said bluntly. "She has her own career, and when I have time, I send for her and she flies to wherever I am."

"It must prove inconvenient for her to have to drop everything when you whistle."

He smiled cynically. "She sees that I make

it up to her. Monette is a very practical lady." He paused. "Does she bother you?"

"Bother me that you have a mistress?" She shook her head. "Why should it? I know last night meant nothing to you. I guess I sort of counted on it."

"How perceptive of you," he snapped. He leaned down and set his cup on the ground. "I suppose you intend to immerse yourself in that icy spring?"

She nodded. "It's not so bad once you get used to it." She finished her coffee in one swallow and set her cup down. "I'll just—" She broke off as he lifted her to her feet and began to unwind the blanket from around her. "What are you doing?"

"Helping you." His expression was enigmatic as he pulled the blanket away and dropped it on the ground, leaving her naked. "You don't mind, do you? After all, seeing you nude means nothing to a hardened womanizer like me." He turned her around and urged her toward the pool with a pat on her fanny that was more of a slap. "Get going. I'll get you a towel and some clean clothes. Where are they?"

"In that trunk over there, but I can—"

"I'll get them," he repeated impatiently. "Get your bath over. You need something to eat."

She hesitated, but he was already striding across the room toward the battered aluminum trunk she had indicated. She turned and walked slowly toward the pool. It felt odd being naked and vulnerable before a man, but Fletch seemed to be completely at ease and as unaffected as he had claimed. Moments later she was standing shivering in the pool, waiting for her body to become accustomed to the numbing cold.

"What's this?" Fletch was coming toward her, carrying the towel, washcloth, and clothes he had taken from the trunk in one hand, and in the other a polished, seven-inch wooden statue. He tossed her the washcloth, dropped the towel and clothes on the stony bank, and held out the statue. "Did you do this?"

She nodded. "That's Paco. Doesn't he have an interesting face? He has an elfin quality."

"At least he's not another Greek god," Fletch muttered. He sat down on the bank and crossed his legs Indian-fashion, studying the statue critically. "This is remarkable. You've brought him to life."

"Thank you. I like it, but Paco says I didn't do him justice." She chuckled reminiscently. "He said his soul was far more handsome than Ricardo's and the eyes of any artist should be able to detect it."

"Did you do one of Lazaro too?"

She nodded as she ran the washcloth over her face and shoulders. "It's in the trunk. Didn't you see it?"

He shook his head. "Is it as good as this?"

"It's better."

His gaze lifted from the statue to her face. "No false modesty. I like that."

"I know I'm good," she said simply. "It started as a hobby, something to make the time pass, but it's not that now."

"Then what is it?"

"Pleasure, excitement, accomplishment. The same thing your work is to you." She shrugged. "I guess 'creative purpose' pretty well encompasses it."

"I guess it does. However, my work affords me a generous living, and sculpting is a career that's hardly lucrative. You do intend to make it a career?"

She nodded. "But I don't need a lot of money." She chuckled. "You'll have to admit that I've had excellent training in doing without for the last six years."

His lips tightened. "All the more reason you shouldn't choose to starve in a garret now that you've finished with St. Pierre."

"But I'm not finished with St. Pierre. Not yet. There's Paco. I'll have time to consider my options later. There's so much I have to do. I'll have to finish my formal education, as well as find a good art school."

He slowly put the statue on the ground beside him. "You still intend to stay here?"

"Of course. There's no reason to change my mind. Paco still needs my help."

"No reason except that you're scared to death. No reason except that you could get yourself killed." His voice was harsh. "Would your precious Paco want you to risk *dying* to get him off this damn island?"

"No, but I have to do it, anyway. Paco is my friend."

"You don't have to do it," he said with barely leashed violence. "All you have to do is hop on that helicopter tonight."

She shook her head, gazing at him in helpless misery.

His hand closed slowly into a fist. "Why do you have to be so damn stubborn? I'm giving you your life. Take it."

"He's my friend," she repeated, dropping her gaze to the water. "Please, I don't want to talk about it. We'll only argue and it will spoil things. We have such a short time before—"

"Spoil things! You're talking as if we have—" He stopped, took a deep breath, and rose to his feet. "Get out of there and dry off."

"I was going to wash my hair."

"Forget it." He strode toward the fire. "It's too cool in here. You'd probably catch a chill."

"I could dry it by the fire."

"Samantha." Fletch's voice was carefully controlled as he took a melon from the bucket and reached for the butcher knife beside it. "I'm trying to hold on to my temper. It would help if you wouldn't argue with me."

She gazed at him uncertainly and then slowly waded out of the pool and began to dry off, her movements quick and efficient. The rough towel was a welcome abrasion against her chilled flesh. She began to dress. "I wouldn't have caught a chill," she said quietly. "I'm used to—"

His voice cut through the sentence with the same sharpness as the knife slicing the melon. "I'm tired of hearing about how accustomed you are to discomfort. You're beginning to bore me."

"Am I?" She tried to keep the hurt from her tone. "I'm sorry. I hope you didn't think I was complaining."

"I didn't think anything," he muttered savagely. "I've discovered it's better not to think when dealing with an idiotic idealist who doesn't know better than to put her neck on the chopping block and letting—" He stopped as his gaze lifted and he saw her face. "And don't look at me like that. It doesn't do a thing to me. You *are* an idiot."

She swallowed hard. "I guess so."

"Well, I know so." He glared at her. "And don't you dare cry."

"I'm not going to cry."

"That's right, big, bad guerrillas never cry, do they? They're too tough. Isn't that what you said? Don't you want to tell me again how tough you are?"

"No." She didn't look at him as she finished buttoning her shirt. "I don't think I do."

"Come over here and eat."

"Okay." She padded barefoot across the cavern and dropped down beside the fire. Her gaze avoided his as she took up the slice of melon he handed her. She stared at it listlessly, knowing she wouldn't be able to swallow a bite until she managed to loosen the knot constricting her throat.

"Why are you just sitting there? Why don't you shout at me?" Fletch asked thickly. "Why don't you tell me to go to hell?"

She shook her head, still not looking at him. "Because I don't want to tell you to go to hell," she said shakily. "I don't know why you're so angry, but I think it's because I might have hurt you in some way."

"So you let me hurt you as some kind of recompense," he said slowly. "How can you be so damn gentle? Don't you have any sense of self-preservation?"

"Yes, but you don't have to hurt someone else to protect yourself. Most people do a pretty good job of hurting themselves without any help." Her eyes were shimmering with unshed tears as she lifted them to gaze at him. "Don't they, Fletch?"

He looked at her for a long moment without speaking. "Oh, God." He tipped up her chin on the curve of his finger, and if she hadn't known better, she would have sworn there was fear as well as aching tenderness in his eyes. "Dear heaven, what am I going to do about you, Samantha?"

"Be my friend," she whispered. "Is that so difficult? I could use a friend right now."

"More difficult than you know." His low voice had a somber ring. "I haven't made a habit of practicing the art of friendship in recent years, particularly with women."

"What a chauvinistic thing to say." She smiled mistily. "Couldn't you try?"

He was silent a moment. "Yes, I can try." His hand fell away from her face. "I don't make any promises, but I'll try, Samantha." He suddenly smiled. "If you'll do me a favor in exchange."

"What?"

He nodded to the slice of melon in her hand. "Eat. Not just a bite or two. I want you to eat like a lumberjack. Will you?"

She nodded happily. She would have done a good deal more to earn again the rare warmth of his smile. "If you'll join me." She bit into the golden fruit of the melon. "It's really very good."

"I can't eat one bite more, so don't tell me I need any more nourishment." Samantha grimaced. "I've changed my mind about you needing a family. You'd probably bully them unmercifully."

"You didn't eat, you nibbled." Fletch scowled. "It's no wonder you're so thin that you're almost invisible."

"I've had enough," she said firmly. "It's still several hours before we can leave for the glade. What do we do now?"

A purely masculine smile curved Fletch's lips. "I thought you'd never ask."

Samantha's breathing quickened. It was

going to happen again, that wonderful, fiery magic. "Yes?"

He reached out and touched her cheek with caressing fingertips. "I suggest we—" He stopped, studying her eager face. The sensuality slowly faded from his expression, and his hand fell away from her face. "What do you usually do to while away the time?"

Samantha tried to mask her disappointment with a careless shrug. "I work on one of my statues or read a book. I have an entire trunk filled with paperback books, if you'd like to take a look at them."

"I don't think so." He stood and picked up the lantern. "I'm restless. I think I'll go exploring. You said there were several other rooms like this one in the cavern?"

She nodded. "You're going away? Perhaps I'd better come with you. You might get lost or—" She broke off when she saw he was shaking his head. She nibbled at her lower lip. "Will you be gone long?"

"I don't know. But don't worry if I'm not back for several hours." He turned away.

"Fletch?"

He glanced at her inquiringly.

She smiled tentatively. "It's just that I thought we might spend some time together today. It would be nice to talk and get to know each other."

His expression was unrevealing. "I don't think that would be a good idea. I'm not feeling very sociable."

"We could play cards. I forgot I had a deck of cards in my trunk."

His gaze searched her face. "What are you trying to say, Samantha?"

She was silent a moment. "Please stay," she whispered. "You'll be gone so soon. I don't want to be alone today."

His expression became even more shuttered. "And what will you give me if I stay?"

"Anything," she said simply.

A muscle jerked in his left cheek. "I know you would, and if I stayed, I'd probably be bastard enough to take whatever was offered."

"There's nothing wrong in accepting gifts."

"No." He smiled cynically. "But there's something definitely shady about accepting bribes. I may play hardball, but I've always tried to play it fair."

"I see." She tried to smile. "I understand. I'm sorry I was so pushy. You must be very bored here, and I'm sure you're sorry you jumped off that helicopter. I told you there was nothing of interest or value on St. Pierre."

"But I think I have found something of value here." He turned slowly to face her. "I'll make a deal with you."

"A deal?"

He nodded. "How many statues do you have here in the cavern?"

Her eyes widened in surprise. "Why just the two heads and three smaller pieces. I gave the rest away when Ricardo sent the men to their homes."

"I want them."

"All of them?" She looked at him in bewilderment. "Why?"

"A whim. I'm a rich man, and I can afford to indulge my whims. What do you want for them?"

She shook her head. "You can have them. I don't want your money."

"You *will* starve in that garret." He groaned. "Don't give away your work. Charge me, dammit."

"All right." She paused. "Stay with me."

Suddenly the silence between them was charged with tension. "You drive a hard bargain," he said slowly.

"I didn't think it was so much. Only a few hours—"

"Harder than you think." He walked toward her and set the lantern back down beside the fire. "But I'm taking what I want, anyway."

"And paying for it?"

"And paying for it." He dropped down beside her. "Through the nose. All right, I'll be your court jester and help you fight your personal dragons. Get that pack of cards, Samantha."

The whir of the helicopter's rotors broke the stillness, and Samantha's hands slowly closed into fists at her sides. It was almost over. In another few minutes the helicopter would be on the ground and Fletch would be climbing into the passenger seat. She would probably never see him again. Pain twisted through her, and she closed her eyes to block out the sight of the slowly descending helicopter. She'd had many partings in her life and this was just another. It wasn't reasonable this one should hurt so much more than the ones that had gone before.

"Samantha?"

She opened her eyes to see Fletch gazing down at her, his expression tense in the moonlight filtering through the trees. "Are you okay?"

"I'm fine." She smiled. "I guess we'd better get out there and meet your pilot."

"In a minute." His gaze was fixed on

her face. "It's your last chance, Samantha. Change your mind and come with me."

She shook her head. "I can't. Not while Paco is still here." She held out her hand. "Good-bye, Fletch. Thank you again for all you've done."

He took her hand. "Just like that?" His voice was suddenly savage. "Good-bye, good luck, have a nice life?"

"What else?" She blinked rapidly to keep the tears from falling. "I doubt if we'll ever run into each other again even if I—" She stopped and wearily shook her head. "We hardly move in the same circles."

"No, we don't." His hand tightened on hers with crushing force. "I can't say I number any martyrs among my acquaintances."

"Don't be angry," she whispered. "You gave me something very special. I don't want to remember you like this."

"How do you want to remember me?" he asked. "The man who stole your last bite of food, not to mention your virginity?"

She flinched. "You stole nothing. Everything was given freely."

"I forgot. Your peculiar ideas of hospitality."

"I didn't realize this would be so difficult." She tried to draw her hand away from his, glancing at the helicopter, which was now hovering only a few feet above the ground. "I think I'd better leave you."

"No!" Fletch's voice was suddenly sharp, and his grasp tightened on her hand. "Come with me to the helicopter." He drew a deep breath, and his tone took on a mocking lightness. "You're so fanatical on the issue of hospitality that at least you can see a guest to the door."

She gazed at him in bewilderment. His demeanor had changed from biting anger to mocking lightness in the flicker of a heartbeat, but she could still sense the disturbance swirling beneath that controlled facade. "If that's what you want."

"That's what I want." His hand released its grip on hers, and he took a step back.

"It's not all that I want, but it will do for a start. I'm learning to do without quite a few things I want since I met you."

She turned away and started across the glade. "Has it been that bad? I know conditions in the cavern were pretty Spartan, but I'd hoped I'd made you comfortable. And we did have a good time this afternoon." During those hours playing cards Fletch had revealed an entirely new facet of his personality. He had been witty, outrageous, even whimsical. She almost wished he hadn't shown her how charming he could be beneath that rough exterior. It made this parting even more difficult. She glanced back over her shoulder. "And you have to admit I did give you something you wanted—those statues in your backpack. They don't have any real value, but you said—"

"They have value," Fletch said, interrupting.

"I'm glad you like them." She smiled. "I like to think of them displayed in one of those fine houses you own. Don't stuff them in a closet somewhere, will you?"

"No, I won't do that."

"Good. Then I'll feel much better about parting with them. Who knows? Maybe someday you'll give a fancy dinner party, a famous art critic will see one of my statues, and I'll be discovered. Perhaps you'll be able to sell them for enough to make it worth the trouble of lugging that load down from the caverns."

"It's worth the trouble now. I have no intention of selling them."

"Then they'll be something to remember me by," she said softly. "I'll like that even more."

An emotion Samantha couldn't identify flickered on Fletch's face before he gave her an equally baffling smile. "I have no intention of remembering you, Samantha."

Hurt tore through her. Stupid. She was so stupid to react like this. Why should he want to remember her? she thought. A fleeting sexual encounter with a clumsy, inexperienced virgin, twenty-four hours of discomfort and danger. "Well, I'll remember you," she said tremulously. "My very first tycoon and my first—oh, God, *run,* Fletch!" She grabbed him by the arm and broke into a dead run toward the helicopter.

A bullet tore past her ear.

"The patrol," Fletch muttered. "They must have sighted the helicopter last night and been waiting for us."

Soldiers were pouring out of the rain forest and thundering across the glade toward them.

They still had several yards to go, but she could see the passenger door of the helicopter being thrown open and heard the engine revving.

Another bullet screamed by her, this one much closer. She cast a desperate glance over her shoulder. A soldier with a drawn pistol was gaining, but he wasn't pointing it at her now. He was aiming at Fletch, the larger target!

"No!" Without thinking, she fell back,

dashing between the soldier and Fletch's broad back. Agonizing pain tore through her, and for a moment she didn't comprehend what had happened. Then she realized she'd been shot. Was she going to die? There was blood...

"God!" Fletch's features were drawn with pain in the moonlight. "Why—" He broke off as Samantha started to crumple to the ground. He snatched her up as if she were a rag doll and covered the last few yards to the helicopter in a desperate sprint.

"Take off!" he shouted as he jumped into the passenger seat.

"The door—"

"To hell with the door!"

The helicopter rose from the ground just as the first soldier reached the open door. The soldier grabbed, missed, then dropped back to the ground, cursing as the helicopter rose another twenty feet and skimmed toward the opposite end of the glade. A spray of bullets hit the metal of the helicopter.

"Cripes," Skip yelled. "I hope they didn't hit the gas tank." He rose another thirty feet, barely skimming the tops of the trees where the glade ended and the rain forest began. "I think we're out of range now. Can you reach over and close that door? Open, it doesn't make for great speed."

Fletch shook his head. "Not yet. I don't want to move her until I find out where she's been hit." His arms tightened around Samantha's slight body. "I'll see if I can stop the bleeding before she regains consciousness."

"Do you think it's bad?"

"How the hell should I know?" Fletch's voice was harsh with pain. "I'm no doctor. She could be dying and I wouldn't be able to tell."

"I couldn't see much in the darkness. Why did she fall back? She could have made it if—"

"She was protecting me. She took the bullet for me." Fletch's mirthless laughter held a thread of desperation. "I should have known she'd do something like this, if she had the chance. I swear the woman has a martyr complex. Dear Lord, she did it for *me*."

Skip cast him a sidewise glance. "She must be a pretty brave woman."

"She doesn't think so." Fletch's hand was trembling as he smoothed back the chestnut hair from Samantha's face. She was as pale as marble in the dim light cast by the control panel. Fear clutched at his throat. Then he saw the faint movement at her temple, and relief pounded through him. She was still alive. "She thinks she's a coward. She was so afraid..." Fletch roused himself and begun to unbutton Samantha's bloodstained shirt. "Get me that first-aid kit under the seat, then radio Damon's Reef and tell them I want a surgeon and a nurse when we land at the heliport."

The shirt was unbuttoned, but he hesitated, his teeth clenched with tension and fear, creating a cold knot in his stomach.

He slowly opened Samantha's bloodstained shirt to examine the wound.

FIVE

THE FIRST OBJECT that came into focus
when Samantha opened her eyes was the
baseball cap. The red, sun-faded hat was
perched with casual impudence on the rum-
pled sandy hair of Skip Brennen. He was
older than he had looked in the shadowy
lights of the helicopter's control panel, she
thought hazily. Brennen must be somewhere
in his mid-thirties, though his square, blocky
physique and lack of height made him appear much younger. Freckles covered his
face in such profusion, they looked like a tan

and formed a solid background for the light blue eyes that were now gazing down at her quizzically. "Hi, I'm Skip Brennen. I won't be hurt if you don't remember me. You were pretty busy the one time we introduced ourselves."

"I remember you . . ." Her eyes widened as she came to full alertness. "Is Fletch—"

"Fletch is fine. You were the only one who was wounded."

She relaxed. "That's good."

"Not according to Fletch." Skip grimaced. "He's been giving us hell for the last twenty-four hours. First he was sure you were dying. Then when he found you only had a graze across your rib cage, he couldn't understand why you wouldn't wake up."

"I don't understand, either." She struggled to a sitting position, flinching as a hot pain streaked through her left side. She shook her head in wonder. Twenty-four hours. She gazed around the light, airy room. This was definitely not a hospital room. Everything around her spoke of the casual elegance that only money and a skilled interior decorator could produce. The room was lovely, summery with its white wicker furniture, the green-leaf print on the white curtains at the large picture windows, the plush luxury of the emerald-green carpet. "Where am I?"

"Damon's Reef. Fletch didn't want you moved any farther until you regained consciousness."

"Moved?" One hand threaded nervously through her hair. "Oh, yes, of course. He'll want to send me to Barbados as soon as I'm able to travel."

Skip shook his head. "Somehow I don't think that's what he has in mind." He grinned down at her. "But I'll let you find out for yourself from Fletch. He told me to let him know the minute you woke up. Do you think you're in good enough shape to face him yet?"

She looked at him in surprise. "Of course. Why shouldn't I be?"

"Well, most people find Fletch a bit over-powering." He tapped his chest. "Yours truly included. I wouldn't want to face him in a weakened condition."

She frowned. "I don't know why you say that. Fletch is really very kind."

"Kind? I don't believe I've ever heard Fletch referred to in that way."

"No, truly. He appears all prickly on the outside, but he does want what's best for people. He just gets crotchety when people don't agree with him about what's best for them."

He burst out laughing. "Crotchety? I love it." He turned away. "I've got to remember to tell Fletch that he's only being 'crotchety' when he decides to smash his next competitor into the dust." There was still a lingering smile on his face as he glanced over his shoulder. "I'll send in your nurse to wash your face and help you brush your teeth." He waved his hand vaguely. "And all that. Fletch didn't want you to wake up to a strange face, so he relegated her to a chair in the hall." He shook his head. "Hell, the only reason he let me sit with you was because he had to take an important transatlantic telephone call."

"Thank you. The nurse's help will be wonderful." She made a face. "I feel terribly untidy."

"You'll feel better soon." He opened the door. "I'll see you later. Okay?"

"Okay."

She watched the door swing shut behind him, then leaned back against the pillows with a sigh of relief. She felt incredibly weak, and it was difficult to sit upright. How stupid to become this helpless from a wound that was hardly more than a graze. But surely she would be perfectly well in a few days, and then she could think about going back to St. Pierre for Paco.

A chill ran down her spine, and she firmly blocked out the fear that was sapping her willpower. It would have been so much better if the patrol had not shown up the previous night. Now she had to steel herself for the task all over again, and there was the additional problem of how she was to get back to St. Pierre. She definitely couldn't let Fletch send her to Barbados. It would be twice as hard to return if Ricardo learned of her intentions.

"Miss Barton?"

She hadn't heard the door open, but a small, heavyset woman in a white uniform stood in the doorway. A brilliant white smile illuminated the woman's café-au-lait face. "I'm Sara London. I know exactly how nasty you feel. You just put yourself in my hands and I'll make you feel one hundred percent okay in the next ten minutes."

The nurse was exuding such bouncy optimism that Samantha found herself returning her smile and permitting herself to relax. She had been surrounded by defeat and despair for so long that it was refreshing to be around a person who had confidence that she could change everything for the better.

"That would be wonderful, Sara. Come in and let's get started."

———

It wasn't until Sara was almost finished with her transformation procedure that Samantha noticed the statues. *Her* statues, all five of the figures she had placed in Fletch's backpack before they had left the caverns, were grouped on a small glass-topped table across the room.

The brush moving through Samantha's hair paused in mid-motion as Sara's gaze followed Samantha's across the room. "They're real nice, aren't they? Mr. Bronson said you'd like to have them here when you woke up. He arranged them on the table himself last night."

Warmth surged through Samantha. "That was thoughtful of him. It's nice to have things familiar to you when you wake up in a strange place." Then she regretfully shook her head. "But they aren't mine any longer. Will you have someone take them to Mr. Bronson?"

"No, she won't." Fletch stood in the doorway gazing at her. Samantha felt her heart leap with delight at the sight of him.

He was dressed in white jeans and a fawn-colored sweatshirt that made his red hair glow flamelike in contrast. The room was suddenly brighter, charged with color and vitality.

"You look a hell of a lot better than you did when I left a little while ago. How do you feel?"

Samantha's amused gaze met Sara's. "One hundred percent okay, thank you. When can I get up?"

"Tomorrow, but even then you'll have to take it easy." He came toward her, his gaze never leaving her face. "For a long time."

She shook her head. "I'll give myself a few days to rest, but I'll be perfectly able to function normally after that." Her gaze returned to the statues across the room. "It was kind of you to have them put here, but you should take them to your room now."

"Oh, should I? As usual, you're leaving me no choice in the matter. Do you have any other instructions for me?" His gaze shifted to Sara. "If you'll excuse us, I think Miss

Barton and I have a few things to discuss privately."

Sara quickly gave Samantha the hairbrush. "I'll be right outside if you need me." She gave Fletch a tentative smile as she hurried from the room.

"Why, she's afraid of you," Samantha said, surprised. It seemed impossible that anyone as confident as Sara could be intimidated, yet that last glance she had shot at Fletch had been definitely apprehensive. "Do you have that effect on many people?"

"I don't know." He shrugged. "That's not important at the moment. I guess I'd better give you a report on your friends to help clear the decks. Lazaro is in a hospital in Barbados. He's doing well and expected to be released in a couple of weeks. I arranged for special help to be given to Luz and any other refugees who might need it. Now let's get to the essentials, shall we?" He dropped down on the cushioned rattan chair beside the bed. "You first. Tell me what your plans are."

"I'll take a few days to recover, and then I'll have to find a way to return to St. Pierre to help Paco." She paused. "I wonder if you might help me with that? Perhaps Skip could drop me off somewhere in the hills. I know it's asking a great deal, but I really can't leave for Barbados yet."

"I have no intention of sending you to Barbados."

"Then could Skip take me to St. Pierre?"

"No, he can't, and since this is a private island, you're not going to find anyone else to take you there, either."

"But I really have to—"

"No." Fletch's hands closed tightly on the arms of the chair. "*Hell,* no. You're not going back to St. Pierre."

"I know you're concerned about me, and it's very kind of you to—"

"I wish you'd stop saying that. I'm not kind," he said impatiently. "I just have the usual amount of horse sense, something you appear to be lacking." He paused. "Besides,

I'm selfish enough not to want you to spoil my plans."

"Plans?"

"I have a few plans of my own, and they don't include you going back to St. Pierre." He held up his hand as she began to protest. "Listen to me. The doctor made all kinds of tests while you were sleeping. He couldn't understand why you collapsed and remained unconscious when the wound was actually minor. He found you were suffering from extreme exhaustion." His hand lowered, slowly closing into a fist. "And malnutrition. He said you'd probably been abusing your body, living on your nerves for years. You need months, not days, of rest. You need good food, long lazy days, and no worry."

She shook her head. "Not now. I'll rest later, after I get Paco off St. Pierre."

"I thought that would be your reaction," Fletch said grimly. "You're like a terrier that won't let go of a slipper. Well, that's all right. It fits into my plans. I have a deal to offer you. You want Paco Ranalto safely off St. Pierre, right?"

She frowned. "Of course."

"And it would endanger your health to go after him right now."

"That doesn't matter. I'm stronger than—"

"If you tell me one more time how tough you are, I'll be tempted to strangle you. I've just spent twenty-four hours sitting here worrying about you."

"Did you worry about me?" Samantha smiled radiantly. "It's nice to have someone worry about me."

He was silent, gazing at her in exasperation. "Even when it's only a 'crotchety' old businessman?"

She laughed. "Skip told you. I did say you could be crotchety, but I never said you were old."

"That's comforting. I'm glad you don't find me completely unappealing. Particularly since my plan calls for considerable intimacy."

She went still. "Intimacy?"

He nodded. "I have a bargain that would meet both our needs. You want your friend, Paco. I want a child with none of the disadvantages I'd ordinarily encounter with a woman who might demand more than I'd be willing to give." He leaned forward, his gaze holding her own. "I propose a trade. I'll send a team of men into St. Pierre to locate both Ranalto and your Dr. Salazar if you like. They'll transport them to Barbados with enough money to set them up quite nicely." He paused. "In return you have my child and agree to sign a document giving me the custody of the child if you decide to leave me. I'd stipulate that you stay with me at least two years after the child is born. I believe that's fair. I heard it's better for the child to have its mother with it during infancy."

"I've heard that too," she said, dazed. This was crazy. She felt as if she were caught in the whirling center of a vortex that was displacing everything that was sane and reasonable. She shook her head to clear it. "You must be joking."

"No, I couldn't be more serious." His gaze moved from her face to the window across the room. "After two years you'd be free to leave. The divorce settlement will be spelled out in detail in the premarital contract. It will be more than generous."

"Divorce? Then you want me to marry you?"

"Of course." His gaze swung back to her in surprise. "Didn't I mention that? If I'm going to go ahead with this, naturally I'll want the child to be legitimate."

"Naturally," she echoed faintly.

"You'll have every comfort, complete freedom, and the knowledge that you helped to free your friends. Doesn't that sound tempting?"

"Yes." She closed her eyes. "It sounds...I don't know. I can't think."

"Open your eyes, Samantha. Look at me." Fletch's voice was gentle. "This is the right thing to do. You know it is. You can trust me."

She opened her eyes to see his face close to hers. His lips were curved in that rare smile that lent beauty to his harsh features. Yes, she could trust Fletch. He was rock-solid in a shifting world. "It wouldn't work, Fletch," she whispered. "I don't think I could give up my child after two years."

"Then you can choose to stay with me," he said calmly. "Or rather, with the child. No one is going to throw you out in the streets. We got along very well in difficult circumstances on St. Pierre. There's no reason we can't be equally companionable on a more conventional plane."

"I seem to remember you were upset with me most of the time on St. Pierre." Her lips were trembling as she tried to smile at him. "We're not at all alike."

"But that doesn't mean we can't enjoy a peaceful coexistence." His gaze returned to the window. "There were a few times when we were in total agreement. You wouldn't have to see much of me. I told you I'm a very busy man."

And he didn't want a wife who would make demands on his time, she thought. Why did that realization bring such pain? "Yes, I remember."

"Perhaps you object to having a child?"

"No, I think I'd like a child of my own. It's been a long time since I had anyone to care about. Except Paco and Ricardo, of course."

"You'll be able to study with the best teachers, and when you're ready, I'll see that your career is launched with the appropriate fanfare. What have you got to lose?"

"I don't know." Her fingers twisted together nervously. "It all seems so ... sterile."

His gaze was on her face immediately. "Do I appear to be a man who would be content with a sterile relationship? I assure you that my appetites are very strong. Or have you forgotten?"

Color flooded her cheeks. "No, but perhaps I won't be able to satisfy you." She tried to keep her voice steady. "You didn't seem to want me after..." She trailed off. This was very difficult. "You may decide I'm not what you want."

"I'll want you. Don't worry about that."

"But I *will* worry about it. I'll worry about everything. This is a crazy idea. You've oversimplified the entire situation. There are so many things that could go wrong."

"I'm not pushing you to make a decision right away." He stood up. "I realize you're still weak and disoriented, and when you do make up your mind, I don't want any backpedaling. Once the deal's made, we push ahead with it."

She laughed shakily. "I feel like the object of a takeover."

He shook his head. "It will be a merger, and the concessions I've offered have been very generous." He suddenly looked uncertain. "I guess I'm doing this pretty clinically, but it's the only way I know how. Do you want pretty phrases?"

"I could use a few words of reassurance."

"But I've told you I'll have a contract drawn up—"

"No, that's not what I mean. Do you *like* me, Fletch?"

A slow smile lit his face. "Oh, yes," he said softly. "There's no question about that. Do you like me?"

She nodded. "Yes, but—"

"No buts." He leaned down to place two fingers on her lips. She inhaled sharply and felt the muscles of her stomach clench. Her lips began to throb beneath his touch, as they had that moment in the caverns. "And no qualifications. Just think about it." His fingers fell away from her lips and he took a step back. "I have to fly to Washington on business, and while I'm there I'll set the wheels in motion to organize a team to get your friends off St. Pierre. I'll be back in two weeks, and you can give me your answer then. All right?"

"All right," she whispered. "I don't know about your . . . your proposition."

"That's why you're going to take this time to think it over." His smile exuded confidence. "It's a good deal and you'd be an idiot not to sign on the dotted line."

"But I'm not a good businesswoman, and I believe you've been rude enough to call me an idiot before."

"That's why you should merge with someone like me." His eyes twinkled. "I'm a whale of a businessman, and I'll make damn sure we make a success of it." He turned away. "Relax, sleep, eat, loll on the beach. If you make a decision before the two weeks is up, tell Skip to phone me and I'll come back."

"You're not taking Skip?"

"He'll fly me to Miami and I'll take a commercial jet from there. I want you to have someone here you know."

"That's not necessary. I can take—"

"Samantha, stop arguing. He's staying." His voice was suddenly weary. "You won't need a nurse after a few days, but you seem to like Sara, so she'll stay on in whatever capacity you decide."

Samantha's lips curved in a faint smile. "Doesn't she have anything to say about it?"

He shrugged. "I'm a rich man. I'll make her an offer she can't refuse."

"You sound like the godfather." She continued deliberately, "And as arrogant as hell."

"I'm not arrogant, but I do know how to get what I want."

"Take what you want and pay for it."

"Exactly." He turned away. "I'll see you in two weeks."

"Fletch . . ."

He glanced over his shoulder.

She gestured to the statues on the table by the window. "You'd better get someone to take them to your room."

He shook his head. "You never give up, do you? But in this case I'm afraid you'll have to resign yourself. Those statues aren't mine. They're yours, Samantha."

"No, we made a deal to—"

He frowned. "For heaven's sake, I wouldn't steal the only things you value just because I caught you at a time when you were vulnerable. What kind of bastard do you think I am?"

She gazed at him in bewilderment. "But why did you bargain for them?"

"Because I knew you cared about them, and it was the only way I could think of to get you to let me take them with me."

"You wanted me to have them, so you schemed to take them *off* the island? That doesn't make sense."

"It makes perfect sense"—he smiled—"when you consider that I never intended to let you stay on St. Pierre. The attack by that patrol made very little difference. You'd still have been on that helicopter when it took off."

"No, you're wrong. I wouldn't have left no matter what you said."

"I'd already exhausted my arguments," he said grimly. "But you would have come with me, anyway."

"Force?"

"If necessary. Though I don't regard saving your neck as kidnapping."

Her eyes widened. "You really would have done that?"

"Yes." He opened the door. "I told you St. Pierre had something I wanted."

"The statues—"

"A woman named Samantha Barton."

The door closed behind him.

Samantha's gaze shifted from the door to stare blindly at the picture of the seascape on the opposite wall. Fletch's last words had shaken her as much as the wild proposition he'd put to her.

It was one thing to accept his philosophy about taking what he wanted, but it was quite another to be the object of his philosophy. Not that he actually wanted her; it was the child he cared about. He merely thought of her as the most suitable and undemanding candidate to give him what he wanted.

She swallowed painfully as the seascape blurred mistily before her eyes. It shouldn't matter to her, she told herself desperately. It wasn't as if she loved Fletcher Bronson. She would never be so stupid or self-destructive that she would let herself fall in love with him. A woman could batter herself against the hard wall of his emotions until she was broken and bloody. He might give her friendship, but little more. Yet there had been moments of exquisite tenderness between them. Didn't that mean there was a possibility his affection could be won, if she tried to be what he wanted?

Dear Lord, she was clutching at straws as if she actually thought he might come to love her. If she accepted his proposition, it would be with the same cool practicality he had shown.

It seemed to be the answer to all their problems. Rescue for Paco and Dr. Salazar, security, and a chance to pursue her studies for herself. It wasn't as if she were searching for love's young dream after all she had been through in the last years. She would probably be stupid to refuse Fletch. It would clearly be the perfect solution for all of them.

She closed her eyes wearily and relaxed against the pillows. Fletch had given her two weeks to make her decision, and there was no need to worry about it until she was stronger. But she would worry about it, she knew. Because if this was such a perfect solution, she couldn't understand why she was experiencing this bewildering premonition of pain to come.

A huge shadow fell across her body, blocking out the strong rays of the afternoon sun. Samantha opened her eyes to see Fletch standing over her. He was only a dark outline framed against the brilliance of the sunlit sky, but there was no mistaking who he was.

"I didn't hear the helicopter." She scrambled to a sitting position on the beach towel. "How are you? Did your business go well?"

"As well as anything goes in D.C." He

squatted down beside her. "How are you?" His keen glance raked over her bikini-clad figure. "Skip said you were eating decently, but you haven't put on much weight."

"It must be my metabolism," she said. "I've always been skinny." His dark blue suit had the stamp of fine English tailoring, and his burgundy-and-gray-striped silk tie was discreet and elegant. He should have looked like the typical, successful businessman, she mused, not a robust Viking. "You look...healthy."

"I'm healthy, you're healthy," he said impatiently. "Now can we get down to business before we also get into Skip's state of health? You sent for me."

She nodded, moistening her lips with her tongue. "I didn't want to bother you, but you told me to let you know when I made my decision."

"You're not bothering me. Tell me."

She hesitated. "I'll do it."

His breath released in a little burst, as if he

had been holding it. A smile lit his rough features. "You won't regret it, Samantha."

"I hope not." Her voice was very low. "I hope neither of us will."

"I won't regret it, no matter how the cards fall." His gaze fell to the gleaming golden flesh of her abdomen. "You don't burn? Skip says you spend most of your time here on the beach."

"My mother was of Italian descent, and I inherited her olive skin." His intent gaze moved to her thighs, and she felt a breathless stirring in the pit of her stomach. "Do you burn?"

He shook his head absently. "You look good in that shade of yellow." He reached out and ran his index finger lightly down her inner thigh. It was the lightest of caresses, yet she felt a streak of fire follow his finger. He must have heard her tiny gasp because he looked up to meet her gaze. "I'd like to see you in a cloth of gold. You'd shimmer like the sun...." He trailed off and seemed to have forgotten what he was saying. A dark flush had mounted to his cheeks, and she could see the rapid pulse at his temple. He pulled his gaze away to look at the waves lapping gently at the shore. "I'll buy you a gown like that someday."

"I have enough clothes." She wanted to reach out and touch him, she realized. She wanted to feel her fingers on the strong brown line of his throat, the bold planes of his face. She hadn't really touched him that night they had been together. Her body might know him sexually, but she had never learned him the way a woman does her lover.

"Nonsense. I sent Skip back from Miami with the bare minimum. I thought you'd prefer to get a complete wardrobe in Paris."

"Paris?" She wished he'd look at her again. She had thought she had caught a glimpse of something hot and basic in his eyes before he had glanced away from her. She couldn't have been mistaken. The at-mosphere between them was still charged with a scorching sensuality that was unmistakable.

Fletch *wanted* her. A swift freshet of joy spread through her in a bubbling tide. She couldn't have been too amateurish that time in the cave, if he still wanted her.

"I thought you'd like to live in Paris. I hear art students are crazy about the ateliers there."

"I never thought about it." What was so fascinating about those blasted waves that he wouldn't look away from them? His hand, braced on the towel beside her, was clenched into a fist, and she found herself fascinated by its power. It was as bold and blunt as Fletch himself, created for action and purpose. Yet she knew that hand could be gentle, those fingers could touch with exquisite gentleness as well as possessive passion.

Slowly, tentatively, she reached out and touched his hand.

He jerked his hand away as if she'd burned him. He stood up abruptly. "Come on." He reached down and pulled her to her feet. "We've got to get back to the villa."

"Now?" she asked, bewildered. "Why?"

He was pulling her along behind him as he strode down the beach toward the large white stucco house. "You said you'd marry me. Let's get to it."

"Today?"

"Why not? We've already wasted a week while you dithered back and forth."

"I did *not* dither." She half ran to keep up with him. "It wasn't something I could decide overnight."

"Well, now that the decision is made, we might as well clinch the deal."

"Where will we be married? Miami?"

He shook his head. "Here. There's a priest waiting in my study."

Her eyes widened. "You brought him with you?"

"Don't get nettled. I wasn't taking you for granted. I just wanted to be prepared in case you decided to honor me with your hand. I don't like to leave my affairs hanging."

"I can see that," she said faintly. She was going to be married. Now. She had never thought much about wedding ceremonies, but she had a vague uneasiness about this lightning-fast ritual. "Fletch..."

He turned to look at her. "Sara and Skip can be the witnesses. There are some dresses in that bunch of clothes Skip brought you, aren't there?"

"Yes, but what about a license?"

"I've got it. I also had your passport renewed and updated and had the premarital agreement drawn up by my lawyers when I was in Washington. Everything's set to roll on greased wheels." He stopped and turned to face her. "Except you. What's wrong, Samantha?"

She gazed at him helplessly. "It's too fast. I feel like I'm being bulldozed into this. You have my head whirling."

"Good, that's how brides are supposed to feel." His smile faded and his expression became grave. "I *want* this, Samantha. I can't remember ever wanting anything as much as I want you to marry me."

"Right now?"

"Right this minute. Will you let me bulldoze you, just this once?"

She hesitated, then slowly nodded. "Very well, but I have an idea it isn't going to be limited to this one time."

His laugh rang out, and for a moment his face reflected a boyish ebullience. "No promises. I've always liked my own way. You'll just have to develop a little aggressiveness to keep me in line. I'll run right over you if you continue to be this gentle."

"Will you?"

His laughter vanished as he leaned forward and kissed her gently, sweetly. "No," he said thickly. "I like you the way you are. There's not been much gentleness in my life, and I value it above price. I'd never try to destroy that part of you." He stroked her hair. "It...moves me."

She laughed shakily, unbearably touched

by his awkward confession. "Even when it annoys you?"

He nodded, his eyes still grave. "Even then." He took a step back and took her hand, threading her fingers through his own. "Remember that next time I start lecturing you." He started off again, his hand companionably linked with hers. "And throw it back at me."

"If I remember correctly, you seldom give me the opportunity to slip a word in edgewise when you're angry with me." She smiled at him. "But I'll work on it."

His eyes held a mixture of tenderness and a strange sadness. "I'll work on it, too, Samantha. I know you're not getting a bargain with this marriage—"

"You're giving me what I want," she said quietly. "And many people would consider it a very good bargain."

He gazed at her a moment. "The team left for St. Pierre two days ago. I don't know how long it will take, but we'll get your friends out, Samantha."

Her eyes widened. "Two days ago. What if I'd said no to your proposition?"

He made no answer.

"You would have done it, anyway," she whispered. "You would have gotten Paco and Dr. Salazar out no matter what I did."

"As a good businessman, I'd be a fool to admit doing something as quixotic as that, wouldn't I? And I'm a very good businessman."

"Yes, you are." Her smile lit her thin face with joyous radiance. "But I like Fletch Bronson, the human being, better. And I happen to think you're an absolutely magnificent human being beneath that IBM-compatible exterior."

"IBM has never found me compatible." The corners of his lips lifted in a smile. "And I doubt if anyone but you thinks of me as a magnificent human being. I do have my own code of ethics, but sending the team had nothing to do with that. It was something I wanted to do, and as I told you once, I always do what I want to do." His smile faded. "Now that you know Paco will be safe and free, you can back out, Samantha."

She shook her head. "I think you know that what you did makes it impossible for me to break my word."

"I hoped it would, but I was too much of a cynic to count on it. I'm not used to trusting people." He paused. "I'll make sure you're not unhappy you made this choice, Samantha. That's a promise, and I always keep my promises."

"So do I." She smiled. "Always, Fletch. Through hell and high water."

For an instant a faint shadow crossed his face. He began walking toward the house in the distance. "Then, by all means, let the nuptials begin."

SIX

THE RING WAS beautiful, an enormous marquise-cut Russian topaz of the finest quality mounted on a gold band studded with diamonds that sparkled brilliantly under the last glowing rays of the setting sun. When Fletch had slipped it on Samantha's finger during the ceremony, she had been stunned. Even now, several hours after the ceremony, it still gave her a little start of surprise whenever she caught a glimpse of it as she moved her hand to reach for her glass of wine.

"Do you like it?" Fletch's glance followed

hcr own to the ring. "I suppose I should have let you pick out something yourself, but there wasn't time. I thought the stone was kind of pretty, and it does match your eyes."

"I love it," she said softly. "I couldn't have chosen anything I liked better." She lifted the glass to her lips and sipped sparingly at the wine. She wanted to keep a clear head that night, and she already felt a little intoxicated with excitement and something else she refused to acknowledge. "But it doesn't look like a wedding ring."

"No, it doesn't." He leaned back in the chair. "And you don't look like a bride." His gaze ran over her melon-colored sundress, lingering on the smoothness of her golden shoulders beneath the spaghetti straps. "Not that I'm complaining. That shade is wonderful with your coloring."

"I didn't have anything that looked bridal, and I didn't think it would matter to you." Her eyes twinkled. "And besides, I wouldn't have wanted to be so elegant that I made Skip feel uneasy. He might have felt obligated to give up his baseball cap in favor of a morning coat."

"Only on pain of death," Fletch said dryly. He suddenly frowned. "He's still calling you Topaz. I told him not to do that."

"Why? It doesn't matter."

"It matters to me. Topaz was part of St. Pierre, and that's all over for you. Now there's only Samantha."

"Well, it shouldn't bother you if it doesn't me." She grinned as she tilted her head to look at him appraisingly. "I wonder how you'd look in a baseball cap? Were you ever a Little Leaguer?"

He shook his head. "I was a bookworm."

She chuckled. "Good Lord, I can't imagine that. You're so . . ."

He lifted one rust-colored eyebrow. "So what?"

"Larger than life."

"Well, I'm larger than several species of life, anyway."

She leaned forward, resting her arms on the table. "Smile."

"What?"

"Smile at me. You have a wonderful smile, but you don't use it enough. You either give me that flinty Easter Island glare or you study me as if I were some weird kind of fauna."

He smiled, and she caught her breath as glowing warmth shimmered through her. "Not at all weird, a very lovely fauna."

"But you *do* study me."

"Yes."

"Why?"

"I guess I just like to look at you," he said simply. "I thought you knew that."

The color rose to her cheeks. "That makes me feel very... bridal."

"You mean, I actually said something right?" He picked up his glass and gave her a half-mocking toast. "We're not exactly the conventional couple, and heaven knows I've certainly not done anything to make this day special for you."

But she *did* feel special, Samantha thought. She felt optimistic and excited and . . . new. It was as if the clock had been turned back to that time before she had learned about war and cruelty, a time when the entire world had seemed as young as she felt that evening.

She suddenly jumped to her feet and kicked off her high-heeled sandals. "I want to go out on the beach. Come with me, Fletch."

He looked startled. "Now? There's something I wanted to talk to you—"

"Now." She was already halfway across the terrace. "I feel *good*. I want to run and laugh and . . ." Her words trailed off as she ran down the flagstone steps from the terrace to the beach.

She was gone, running down the beach, her full skirts flying in the wind, her dark hair shimmering with fire as the rays of the setting sun bathed her in their pink-red glow.

Fletch slowly rose to his feet, his gaze following her. He had never seen Samantha like this. He hadn't fully realized the dark shadow that had always clung to her until this moment when she had cast it off and was completely free. There was no shadow now. She was flaming with vitality, and he suddenly knew this was how she was meant to be.

She turned around and waved. "Come on. What's wrong?"

"Nothing." He took off his jacket and tossed it on the chair. "Not one damn thing. Wait for me."

She stood there until he joined her, and then started out at a half trot again. "I like your island, Fletch. And I like your beach and your house, and your ocean…"

He laughed as he caught her hand, keeping pace with her. "I can't lay claim to the ocean. And I think you've gone a little crazy. What's gotten into you?"

"I don't know." She turned to face him, walking backward, her eager gaze on his face. "Or maybe I do. I think it's hope, Fletch. I think I have hope."

"Hope for what?"

"Oh, I don't know. Life. Happiness." She gestured helplessly. "Everything. It's been so long since I dared to think about anything but the next minute, the next hour. But now I can actually make plans for next *year*. It seems like a miracle."

An unbearable surge of tenderness tightened his throat. "Does it, Samantha?"

She nodded. "I have a future." She suddenly stopped. "And you're a part of it." She took a step closer and slipped into his arms with supreme naturalness. "I want to *know* you, Fletch. You're going to be very important in my life."

His arms tightened around her. "I think we know each other better than most married couples. At least, I know you. There's not much to know about me. What you see is what you get."

"I don't think that's true. I think there's a great deal more to you than what's on the surface." She looked at him thoughtfully. "Every time I turn around, I learn something new about you. Talk to me. Where were you born? Where did you grow up? Were you close to your parents?"

"Hold it." He chuckled indulgently. "Give me a chance. I was born in Seattle, Washington, and I grew up in a suburb there. My father owned a small electronics plant. My mother was an engineer and worked very closely with him. They made a great team." His smile faded. "My mother died when I was in college, my father three years later."

"You were close?"

"Not particularly. They were...busy."

Her expression softened. "I'm sorry. That must have been very difficult for you. A child needs—"

"Don't waste your sympathy on me," he said, interrupting. "You don't miss what you've never had. I wasn't a victim, though I was undoubtedly an accident they were forced to tolerate. Maybe my parents were workaholics who never should have had children, but I can't fault them when I run my life the same way."

"But you want a child."

He nodded. "And I'll be a good father. I won't cheat—" He stopped, surprised. "Hell, maybe I do see myself as some kind of a victim. I didn't think I was self-pitying."

"You're not." She felt a tenderness that was almost maternal. No wonder he had erected such a high wall around his emotions. How many rejections had he suffered before he had been forced to emulate his parents and substitute ambition for emotion? Yet there was nothing unemotional about the Fletcher Bronson she had come to know. He was full of anger and passion and caring. "But I think you're wise to have decided to have a child to complete your life. You need it." She stood on her tiptoes and pressed a kiss as light as a summer breeze on his lips. "Just as I do. I'll give you a child we can both love, Fletch."

He gazed down at her, a multitude of emotions chasing across his face. "You don't look much more than a child yourself," he finally said gruffly. He reached out and tugged playfully at a strand of her chestnut hair. "And I feel like a dirty old man." He took a step back and released her. "I have to make a few phone calls. We'd better get back to the house."

"Now?" She couldn't keep the disappointment from her voice.

His smile was bittersweet. "I'm not twenty-one and full of hope and visions of the future. I'm thirty-seven and weighed down with years and responsibilities." He took her elbow and began to guide her gently in the direction of the villa. "It's one of the crosses you'll have to bear as my wife. I have a merger pending, and I'm going to be under constant pressure for the next few months."

"I understand." She didn't look at him. "I didn't mean to...I know we have an agreement. I'll try not to interfere."

"For heaven's sake, Samantha, this is your wedding day. I should be the one apologizing."

She tried to smile. "But this isn't the usual

wedding day, is it?" Her eyes slid away, and the words tumbled out feverishly. "I know how busy you are. It was very kind of you to spend this much time with me. It was silly of me to think it could be any different. Oh, look, my feet are all sandy." They had reached the steps, and she pulled away from him and ran up the steps. "I'll just go to my suite and wash them. I'll see you later, Fletch. I hope those business calls go well."

She quickly disappeared through the French doors into the house.

Fletch stood still on the terrace, his hands clenching into fists at his sides. He had hurt her. He had robbed her of the radiance of happiness and hope; he had brought her back into the shadows. Damn, he hadn't wanted to hurt her. If he hadn't been so clumsy...

But he *was* clumsy, he thought grimly. He would blunder and hurt her, neglect and probably destroy her, if given the chance.

He moved slowly, heavily, toward the French doors. He had to talk to Skip and

Sara, and then he badly needed a drink. He wished to hell there really were some earth-shaking phone calls he had to make. It would have kept him from remembering Samantha's face that moment before she had run into the house. It would have kept him from thinking of the note he had to write to give Sara for Samantha.

Rats, she looked about as voluptuous as Little Orphan Annie, Samantha thought in supreme discontent as she twisted and turned before the full-length mirror. Champagne beige was a good color for her, but that was all the nightgown had going for it. She made a face at her image in the mirror. What had she expected, for goodness sake? Expensive lingerie couldn't give someone like her the earthy appeal of a woman like Monette Santore. Unfortunately one had to have some curves to put into a nightgown to make it sexy.

She turned away from the mirror with a

sigh of discouragement. She wished she hadn't thought about Monette Santore. She was nervous enough tonight without worrying about Fletch's former mistress.

Former? She stopped in mid-motion as she was reaching for her negligee, draped on the back of the rattan chair. How did she know the actress was relegated to Fletch's past? There had been no clause in that contract she had signed that guaranteed his fidelity, and he had never given her any assurance he wouldn't send for any woman who caught his eye whenever it pleased him. Why should he be satisfied with a wife who wasn't as sexy or experienced or—She had to stop this, she told herself as she slipped on the negligee. There. She didn't look nearly as bad with her bony shoulders covered. Maybe he wouldn't notice in the dark how skinny she was. Still, it hadn't been dark in the cave, and he hadn't seemed to think she was too ugly. Perhaps it would be all right. Oh, Lord, she was nervous. Nervous and excited and—

There was a soft knock on the door. Fletch?

"Come in." Her voice sounded quavery even to her.

Sara opened the door. "Hey, you look real pretty. Like one of those ads in *Vogue*. Do you want me to brush your hair?" She bustled into the room. "You've had a big day. Now why don't you let me tuck you into bed?"

"Not yet. I'm waiting..."

Sara stopped in the center of the room, her eyes widening in surprise. "Mr. Bronson gave me a letter for you, but I thought you knew." She hurriedly reached into her pocket and brought out a folded piece of stationery. She crossed the room and thrust the note into Samantha's hand. "You call me if you need me." She turned and hurried toward the door. "And don't you stay awake worrying about any of this. You need your rest."

"Sara?"

Sara turned reluctantly at the door.

"What did you think I would know?"

Sara's gaze fastened on the note in Samantha's hand, carefully avoiding her eyes. "That Mr. Bronson and Mr. Brennen took off in the helicopter for Miami forty-five minutes ago. It's probably in that note he wrote you. I guess he was in a big hurry and didn't have time to..." She trailed off and quickly opened the door. "You call me if you need me." The door closed behind her.

Poor Sara, Samantha thought dully. She had been so embarrassed and distressed at having to be the bearer of bad news. It wasn't every day a third person had to inform the bride that the groom had literally flown from the bridal nest.

She slowly unfolded the note. The note was terse, to the point, and typically Fletch: "Samantha, I'll call you from Miami to explain. Take care of yourself. Fletch."

Take care of yourself. How very tender and loving, she thought as a shiver of pain radiated through her. But she wasn't entitled to either love or kindness from Fletch. That wasn't in their agreement. Those business calls he'd had to make had evidently generated a fascination more urgent than his desire to sire a child. Certainly more urgent than his desire for her.

Oh, well, she didn't care. It didn't matter. She had no right to demand anything from Fletch.

Her hand slowly clenched around the paper, wadding it into a tight ball. If she had no right, then why was she hurting so much? And if she didn't care, why did those brief words strike like acid-dipped needles?

She dropped the note on the floor and moved slowly toward the French doors that led to the terrace. He would be calling soon. Fletch always did what he said he would do. When he called, she must be controlled and calm. She mustn't let him know.

Know what? She had been hiding, dodging the truth for so long that it was now obscure, veiled even from herself. But there always came a time to lift the veil. She had been a coward too long.

She opened the French doors and breathed in the warm salty air. The night was soft and sensuous; the sound of the waves rushing onto shore had an alluring rhythm. She must ignore both the sensuality and the allure. She moved toward the cushioned rattan chair and sat down, her slim hands clutching its smooth braided arms. She had to think. When Fletch called her, she must not be in this turmoil. She must know.

It was over an hour later when the phone rang.

Samantha rose and moved quickly from the terrace to the bedroom extension and lifted the receiver. "Hello?"

"Samantha?" Fletch's voice was quick and vibrant. "Did I wake you?"

She almost laughed aloud. "No, I was waiting for your call."

"Damn, that was a stupid question." There was silence on the other end of the line. "I don't have much time. My plane leaves in fifteen minutes. I'm sending Skip back to the island tomorrow morning."

"That's not necessary." Her voice was steady, she noted with a sense of pride. "I don't need him here. I'll be fine until you get back."

"You're not going to stay at the villa. Skip is going to escort you to Paris and stay with you until you're settled into the château."

Her hand tightened on the receiver. "If that's what you want. When will you join me there?"

There was another pause. "Not for some time."

She tried to laugh. "Unless you're thinking of a test-tube baby, I understand it's a little difficult to conceive a child long-distance. Or do you intend to send for me when you have time? The way you send for Monette Santore?"

He muttered something beneath his breath that sounded faintly obscene. "No, I thought—" He stopped. "I decided it would be better to wait until you're stronger. You have no business becoming pregnant until you're entirely well."

Relief poured through her, and with it a rising fountain of joy. He had been thinking of *her*. Surely that must mean he felt something for her. "But I feel wonderfully healthy," she said eagerly. "I'm starting to put on weight, and I'm rested and—"

"No," he said, interrupting. "It will be better for you and the child if we wait. So we wait."

Dear heaven, this was difficult. "I could still come to you."

"I'll be busy in the next few months," he said evasively. "It will be better if you stay at the château and start your lessons. There's no hurry."

"No, there's no hurry," she repeated dully. "You're a very patient man. I suppose I should thank you."

"You're remarkably lacking in enthusiasm." He paused. "Did I hurt you that much, Samantha?"

"No, why should—" She broke off. She wouldn't lie to him. "Yes, you hurt me." She cleared her throat to ease the painful tightness. "I didn't realize I was so egotistical, but you have to admit it's a little unflattering to have a man go to these lengths to avoid making love to you."

"Don't talk hogwash," he said roughly. "You turn me on more than any woman I've ever met. Don't you realize that? I nearly went crazy when I was loving you. I ache even thinking about how good it was moving in—" He heaved a sigh. When he spoke again, his voice was deliberately light. "You don't have to worry about whether I want you, if that's all that's bothering you." When she didn't answer, he asked quietly, "Samantha?"

"That's what was bothering me," she whispered. He had enjoyed her body. He wanted her. That could be a lot to build on. "Thank you for telling me."

"Samantha, for heaven's sake..." He was silent a moment. "I have to go now. I'll make arrangements for my lawyers in Paris to give you an allowance for personal expenses. The bills for the château are sent to them as a matter of course. If you need anything at all, just ask Skip."

"All right."

"One more thing. I'm going to make sure news of our marriage doesn't leak to the press. It will make it safer for you to move around Paris freely if you're not known as my wife. There are all kinds of kooks who slime out of the woodwork when they scent money."

"Okay."

"Samantha, you did the right thing in marrying me. Just leave everything to me and you won't be sorry."

"Good-bye, Fletch. You mustn't miss your plane."

"Good-bye, Samantha."

The soft click of the receiver brought silence and loneliness to the room.

She slowly replaced the receiver and stood looking at the ivory-colored phone without seeing it. She had been plunged from nervousness to depression to hope so quickly in the last few hours that she felt dazed.

He wanted her. She had a chance. Marriages like the one they had entered into weren't really all that unusual. In medieval times, and for centuries later, there had been marriages contracted purely for reasons of convenience. Love often had to come later. She could build on passion and desire as those ladies of the past had done. But she must be very careful. She must not be demanding or make Fletch feel guilty. That would be a terrible mistake.

And she must never let him know how she felt about him.

No, above all, she must not let Fletch know how much she loved him.

SEVEN

"IF YOU WON'T give up this life in a garret for yourself, think of me," Skip complained as he stretched out his legs in front of him and gazed gloomily at the statue of Fletcher Bronson that Samantha was working on. "Fletch won't let me go back to New York until you move to the château, and I can't stand this blasted city. Parisians don't like Americans."

"I've never noticed that." Samantha took a step back and tilted her head to one side.

"What do you think, Skip? Are the cheekbones a little too broad?"

"No, they're fine. That's Fletch, all right." He glanced away from the statue and back to Samantha to argue, "And the only reason you never noticed Americans are on the Gallic blacklist is that you have a sort of cosmopolitan air. Most of the time they don't even know you're an American. If they pretend they don't understand English, you chatter at them in Spanish. Now when they look at me, they zero in for the kill."

"Nonsense, Parisians are perfectly wonderful." Her lips twitched as she gave him a sidewise glance. "But if you don't want to be recognized as an American, you could get rid of that baseball cap. It's a dead giveaway."

"Give up my cap?" He gazed at her in outrage as he gave the bill of the cap a protective tug. "No way, that's carrying things too far."

Samantha's eyes danced with amusement. "Just a thought."

"A damn bad one," Skip said in a voice like a growl. "Like living in this crummy studio, five flights up. I nearly have a heart attack by the time I reach your front door. It's idiotic to live here when you could be lolling in luxury at the château."

"The light is wonderful here." She motioned to the skylight above her. "And my studio is not crummy. It's clean and neat and—"

"It looks like a nun's cell," Skip said, interrupting her. "And the radiators don't work half the time, and it's *five* flights up."

She laughed. "I thought you liked heights, Skip. After all, you're a pilot."

"I like flying," he said flatly. "That's entirely different. Flying doesn't require exercise that would kill a horse. You know damn well that Fletch wouldn't like it if he knew you'd rented this place, Topaz. I don't know why I ever let you talk me into letting him think you were living in a decent apartment."

"That's why you're not going to tell him.

Though this is a decent place. My neighbors are all artists and very friendly, and it's close to the school. It's certainly all I need right now. I don't do much but work, anyway."

"You don't do *anything* but work." Skip shook his head. "I thought you'd want to break loose and have some fun after what you went through on St. Pierre."

"I am having fun." She looked back at the statue. "I go to museums and coffee shops with the other students, and I work. That's the most fun of all."

"You're hopeless." Skip grimaced. "And a little crazy. You're married to one of the richest men in the world, and you live like a pauper. You scarcely touch the allowance Fletch gives you. In the last four months you haven't bought any clothes or shelled out the money for a respectable place to live. You wouldn't even eat enough if I didn't come in every day and remind you."

"Do I look as if I'm suffering?"

"No," Skip admitted reluctantly. "You

look . . ." He paused, trying to see her objectively. It was a difficult thing to do. He'd grown too close to her in the past months. Topaz hadn't put on much weight, but her skin no longer had that transparency he had noticed the first time he had seen her. The tension that had shadowed her every moment was gone too. She wasn't blooming with exuberance and vitality, but there was a glow, a quiet serenity, and a strength that appeared to be growing, deepening, with every passing day. "You look good."

"Then stop worrying about me and tell Fletch I'm doing very well."

"You could tell him yourself, if you'd get a telephone."

"Stop nagging, Skip. You can't expect me to adjust to all these newfangled ideas after six years in the hills. It's very peaceful being out of touch when you want to be."

Skip's expression became grave. "Well, you're not going to be out of touch for much longer. Fletch is flying in from New York tomorrow evening."

Samantha quickly averted her face. "Really? The merger is done?"

"I don't know, but he said there were some loose ends he had to attend to in person here."

"Like me?"

Skip hesitated. "I don't suppose you'd like to tell me what's between the two of you? This marriage is weird as hell."

Samantha shook her head. "Maybe someday."

"But I'd bet it has something to do with why you're determined to accept so little from Fletch and went out and got yourself that part-time job modeling at the atelier?"

"I like the job, and it pays extremely well for only a few hours a week."

"You're being evasive."

She gave him a fleeting smile before turning back to the statue. "Right."

"Oh, well, I didn't think you'd tell me." Skip sighed. "No one tells me anything. All Fletch said on the phone was that he's having a big party at the château tomorrow evening, and he wants to see you before it starts." His gaze traveled over her faded jeans, Docksiders, and stained T-shirt. "Do you suppose you could force yourself to spend some of Fletch's money on a gown? If you show up like that, he's going to have some very touchy questions to ask about why I haven't been taking care of you."

"You've taken very good care of me." Her tone was abstracted as she stared blindly at the statue in front of her. Tomorrow night. She would see him tomorrow night. These last four months had seemed like an eternity. Yet in a way she had welcomed the separation. She had needed time to establish her own roots, to get to know herself as a person as well as an artist, and she had begun to do all those things. She had gained confidence. In spite of Skip's skepticism, it had been an exciting period for her.

But not like this excitement... this exhilaration... hunger, brilliance, comets streaking through space. Fletch. "And, yes, I'll buy a gown." She turned toward him, a glowing smile on her face. "I'll even let you take me shopping tomorrow morning. I'm sure Dior will adore your baseball cap."

"Let me in," Skip said, gasping as he pounded on the door. "Quick."

Samantha tightened the belt of her robe as she hurried across the room and threw open the door. "You're not dressed. Aren't you going to the party?"

"No way." Skip was panting and clutching at the frame of the doorway, struggling to get his breath from the long trek up five flights of stairs. "I'll drive you to the château and then go out to the garage. Pierre, Fletch's chauffeur, runs the classiest floating crap game in Paris. I bet I'll have a helluva better time than you will." He reached into his pocket and pulled out a long black jeweler's case. "Fletch sent this. I think I can make it to a chair now." He shoved the leather case into her hand as he kicked the door shut and dropped into his favorite easy chair a few feet away. "I'm glad you're not dressed yet. It'll give me time to rest. Tell me, if I find you a *pension* that's just as cheap on a ground floor someplace, will you *please* move?"

She shook her head. "The light." She opened the box. Russian topaz and square-cut diamonds alternated on a bracelet of unsurpassed beauty that shimmered with exotic richness under the overhead lights. "It's magnificent." She took the slender strand out of the box. "But I'd be afraid to wear it. It looks as if it would slip off my wrist."

Skip shook his head. "It goes on your upper arm. I think it's a sort of slave bracelet. When I described your gown, Fletch phoned a jeweler in town and told him what he wanted, and I picked it up on the way here." Skip's gaze traveled over her robe clad figure. "You'd better get a move on. The party is at nine, and Fletch said he'd like you in the study by eight so that you'll have time to talk."

"I only have to put on my gown." She went behind the screen. "I needed someone to help me with the zipper." She tried to keep her voice casual. "You saw Fletch?"

"I met him at the airport."

"How is he?"

"He's Fletch," Skip said simply. "He never changes. Mr. Powerhouse Incorporated. He looks tired, though. He's probably been working himself into the ground with this merger."

"Did he mention me?"

"No, and I avoided the subject like the plague. It's one thing to evade his questions on the telephone, but it's an entirely different matter to have to do it to his face. Thank heavens he seemed absorbed with these manufacturing kingpins he's wining and dining tonight."

"Fletch told me once he didn't like parties. Why is he giving one tonight?"

Skip shrugged. "Search me. He does hate entertaining, but the French like to combine business and pleasure. He must want something pretty badly from these tycoons to go to all this trouble." He glanced at his watch. "It's getting late. Are you nearly ready?"

Samantha closed her eyes. Was she ready? She wasn't at all sure now that the moment had come. Her hands were trembling, her palms moist, and her heart was racing like a runaway train. She felt as she had that night in the cave, fearful of the future, an uncertain child in a world she wasn't sure she understood.

But she wasn't that child any longer. She was a woman, and it was time she started acting like one. She stepped from behind the screen. "I'm ready." She smiled. "Or I will be, as soon as you fasten this blasted zipper."

Fletch hadn't expected her to look so sophisticated.

Samantha, standing in the doorway of the

study, resembled a high priestess in some ancient temple dedicated to the sun god. Her gown left one shoulder bare in the Grecian fashion, and the shimmering gold fabric draped and molded her slim body with a consummate artistry that was both sensual and completely feminine. Her hairstyle was different, too, a long, lustrous flip that, though simple, also displayed a certain sophistication.

He stood up and came around the desk. "You look beautiful, Samantha. I told you that cloth of gold would become you." Beautiful but...different, he thought with a pain that was curiously nostalgic. His lips brushed her cheek, and he caught a faint, spicy fragrance. He could feel the sudden heat of arousal rush to his loins. So he still couldn't be in the same room with her without wanting to pull her down on the floor and push up her skirt.

He blocked the thought and quickly stepped away from her. He had been hoping that time would cool, or at least temper, his desire for her. It would have helped to be able to think with his head instead of the other part of his anatomy that persisted in dominating him whenever she was close. "And the arm band goes quite nicely with your gown. I hoped it would."

"Thank you, it's lovely. I feel like a barbarian princess wearing it." She moistened her lips with her tongue. "It's good to see you, Fletch. How have you been?"

A smile tugged at the corners of his lips. "This sounds familiar. Are we going to begin a health discussion again?"

"No." She smiled, too, feeling more at ease. "It's not necessary. I can see that you're tired but won't admit it. And I'm completely well, so that's the end of the discussion." She met his eyes directly and repeated deliberately, "Completely well, Fletch."

His gaze slid away from her. "I can see that." He turned away abruptly. "It's damn close in here. Let's go out on the terrace." He strode toward the doors and threw them open. "Skip says your studies are going full steam ahead. How do you feel about it?"

"Good." She followed him out on the terrace, pausing a moment to enjoy the sheer magic of the view. Moonlight touched the formal rose garden before her with a silver radiance and gave the towers and battlements of the château a fairy-tale beauty. "Good heavens, this is lovely." She stood for a moment drinking in that loveliness before crossing the terrace to where he was waiting by the balustrade. "What were we talking about? Oh, yes, my studies. I'm learning a lot about a great many things, but principally how much I have to learn about nearly everything."

"That doesn't appear to intimidate you." His gaze narrowed on her face. "You've changed."

"Perhaps I've grown up a little." A gamin smile lit her face. "There was room."

"More than a little," he said slowly. "You're ... different."

"If you say so." She shrugged impatiently. "But I don't think you brought me here to tell me this. You're a busy man, as you've said many times before. Why am I here, Fletch?"

"I received word two days ago that your friend Paco Ranalto, Dr. Juan Salazar, and their families arc off St. Pierre. They're now in Barbados, and I'll arrange to have them transported to the country of their choice and resettled as soon as possible."

Samantha stood frozen as relief streamed through her. "Thank God."

He nodded. "It's all over. Your friends are safe."

"Oh Fletch, do you know what this means to me?" Her eyes were sparkling with tears of joy as she reached out a hand to grasp his arm. "It's like...I don't know." She spun away from him in a giddy circle. "It's *wonderful*. It's a new beginning for all of us."

"I'm glad you see it that way," he said gently. "That's what I wanted for you. A new beginning, Samantha." He paused. "With no strings."

Her smile faded. There was a significance beyond the obvious in his words that she couldn't mistake. "What do you mean?"

"I mean, I'm having our marriage annulled." He looked away from her out over the garden. "Very quietly. With any luck no one will ever know it existed. Your allowance will continue until you can support yourself decently, and of course there will be a settlement that will—"

"I don't understand," she said in bewilderment. "We have an agreement."

"It's over. Your friends are safe now."

"But I haven't fulfilled my part of the bargain."

He didn't answer her.

"You never intended me to repay you," she whispered. "No wonder you made sure the newspapers didn't find out about our marriage. It was all lies."

Fletch swung around to face her, and she was shocked at his tormented expression.

"What did you expect me to do? I *know* you. I never could have stopped you from going back to St. Pierre for Ranalto. I had to set up a situation you would accept to let me do the job for you."

"Not like this." Her voice was shaking. "You shouldn't have done it like this."

"How else?" he asked hoarsely. "I didn't have much choice. I won't lie to you. I'd do it again if presented with the same circumstances. There's no way I'd let you go back into danger."

"*Let* me? It's my life. Do you know how I feel? How can I have any respect for myself if I let you do this?"

"For God's sake, you took a bullet for me, Samantha," Fletch said roughly. "If you want to talk about debts, that should pay me in full."

"No, it's not the same." Her eyes were glittering in the moonlight. "You wouldn't even have been on St. Pierre that night if it hadn't been for me. We made a deal, and now you're backing out of it."

"Hell, yes, I'm backing out of it. Do you think I'm going to take anything else from you? I've been taking since the moment I set eyes on you. Lord, I almost took your *life*. If that bullet had been an inch closer, you would have died on St. Pierre." His light eyes were blazing with intensity as he looked down at her. "So don't tell me I have an obligaton to make a brood mare out of you, because I just won't buy it. You'll take your freedom and the settlement."

"No, I—"

"Samantha, don't do this to me. Do you think this is easy? For once in my life I'm trying not to think of myself. Help me."

She gazed at him, finding it difficult to think, her mind clouded by pain and bewilderment. No, she could see it wasn't easy for him. Deep lines of suffering grooved either side of his lips, and his eyes held the same torment she was experiencing. Perhaps she should try to understand and sympathize with him, but instead she felt a sudden flare of fierce anger. "I don't feel like helping you at the moment. I feel like kicking you."

A flicker of surprise crossed his face. "I suppose I can understand that."

"Can you? I'm beginning to think you don't understand anything about me." She took a step back, crossing her arms over her chest to ward off a sudden chill that had nothing to do with the balmy weather. "You're mistaken, Fletch. You don't know me."

"Samantha—" He took an impulsive step toward her and then stopped. "You're upset right now, but once you think about it, you'll realize it's for the best. Do you want me to have Skip drive you home?"

She shook her head. "I believe I was invited to a party."

He frowned. "Are you sure that—"

"I'm sure," she said curtly. "Don't worry, I won't embarrass you. I've learned a few social amenities since I left the caverns."

"I never said—" He broke off and shook his head. "If you said that to hurt me, you've succeeded. You could eat with your knife and swing from the chandelier and it wouldn't matter to me." His smile was bittersweet. "I'd probably enjoy it. I hate these stuffy shindigs."

Samantha felt a rush of tenderness that came close to submerging the hurt she was experiencing. She wished desperately that she could stop the tenderness, stop the loving, but she was afraid it would never leave her now. "I'm afraid you'll be disappointed, then. I was my father's hostess from the time I was twelve years old. There won't be any chandelier swinging."

"Pity." One blunt finger reached out to touch her cheek. "I think I'd enjoy seeing gentle little Samantha do something wild."

"Would you?" She stepped back from him because she wanted that touch so badly. She had forgotten how hot and weak she became when he was so close. "Perhaps someday I'll oblige."

"Not you. You're too—"

"Gentle," she finished for him. "It's getting late. Your guests will be arriving."

It was a clear dismissal, and for a moment he was disconcerted. She had changed from quivering emotionalism to cool serenity in the space of moments. "Let me take you inside."

"No, I want to stay out here for a while. I'll be in later."

"I don't think that would be a good idea."

"I do," she said calmly. "Don't worry, there won't be any weeping and wailing. I just have some thinking to do. Run along."

He found himself staring at her in bemusement before turning away.

"Oh, I do have three questions I'd like to ask you if you don't mind."

He glanced back over his shoulder. "I don't mind."

"Is Monette Santore still your mistress?"

He shook his head. "I haven't seen her since I left for St. Pierre."

She carefully kept from her expression

any hint of the relief she was feeling. "Do you have another mistress?"

"Samantha, this is..." He shook his head again. "No."

"Did you really want me, or was that a lie too?"

He looked away from her, and she thought he wasn't going to answer. Then the words came slowly, haltingly. "It was no lie. I want you."

He turned, and his stride as he left the terrace and entered the château possessed a strange element of flight.

Want, not wanted. Present, not past tense. Hope.

The faintest smile touched Samantha's lips as she looked out over the garden. She stood there for a long time, a slim goddess of the sun in a realm of moonlight.

Then, her decision made, she turned and walked briskly across the terrace and entered the château.

EIGHT

IF SHE DIDN'T do it now, she never would.

Samantha braced herself and opened the door to Fletch's suite. Her breath escaped in a little rush of relief as she saw that he wasn't in the sitting room. She had thought she was ready to face him but found the reprieve more than welcome.

"What the devil do you mean, you didn't take her home? Who else would do it? One minute she was standing in a corner talking to Frezdorf, and the next she was gone." A door to the left of the elegant sitting room was ajar, and Fletch's impatient voice was issuing from what must be the bedroom.

"No, Frezdorf didn't take her home. He stayed to talk to me after the party."

Only one voice. He must be talking to someone on the phone, she thought as she moved toward the door.

"Well, find out where she is. Go to her apartment and make sure she's all right."

Another pause and then Fletch spoke again, enunciating each word with great clarity. "I don't care if it's after three in the morning, Skip. I want to know she's safe. You should have insisted she get a telephone. Who ever heard of anyone not having a telephone in this day and age?"

Poor Skip. Fletch was giving him too much flak for her to stand here hesitating just because she was suddenly assaulted by a case of nerves. She pushed open the door. "It's very peaceful without a telephone jangling at you all the time."

Fletch was sitting upright, his auburn head leaning back against the exquisitely carved mahogany headboard of the canopy bed. He was completely naked.

Relief flickered across his rough-hewn features as he saw her standing in the doorway. Then it was gone, and his face was expressionless once more. He spoke into the phone. "Never mind, Skip, it's okay." He hung up the receiver. "I suppose you have some explanation for worrying the hell out of me?"

"Were you worried? I didn't mean to trouble anyone." She came into the room and closed the door. "I just wanted to simplify matters, and I thought this was the best way to do it."

She hadn't expected him to be naked. The sight of him gave her an odd erotic shock. In the primitive earthiness of the cavern she had found the nudity of his bold, powerful body arousing but somehow natural. In this ultra-civilized room of Louis XIV furniture and delicate patterns carved on fine old wood, his sexuality was a stunning anomaly. Her gaze was drawn like a magnet to the brawny muscles of his thighs, framed against the navy satin sheets.

"Of course I was worried." He scowled. "All evening you were laughing and talking, charming every blasted man in sight, and then you disappear completely."

"I was waiting on the terrace until the last of your guests left." She smiled faintly. "I did some scouting earlier to locate your suite. I'm quite good at scouting, you know. It's a talent I was forced to acquire in the last six years."

"May I ask why I'm honored by your presence? I thought you understood my position and that our discussion was finished."

"Oh, I'm done with discussion." She kicked off her shoes, reached behind her, and unzipped her gown. "Talk is entirely finished." She let the gown drop to form a golden pool on the Aubusson carpet. She stepped out of it, dressed only in a garter belt, her bikini panties, and the sheerest of stockings. "I understood everything you said."

Fletch's gaze was fastened, mesmerized, on the delicate fullness of her naked breasts. "What the hell do you think you're doing?" he asked hoarsely.

"Undressing." She sat down on the petit-point-cushioned seat of the Louis XIV chair against the wall and unfastened one of the tabs holding her stockings. "I thought that was obvious."

"Samantha, listen—"

"No," she said clearly, rolling down the stocking and pulling it off. "You listen to me." She undid the other stocking and started to roll it down. "You made sure I was put in a position where I was forced to accept your charity—"

"It wasn't charity. You were shot because of me, dammit."

"It was charity." She tossed the stocking aside and unfastened the garter belt. "And it only goes to show how little you really know me, that you'd even think I'd let you get away with it."

"I do know you. You get to know someone pretty well under circumstances like the ones we shared."

She shook her head. "You got to know only a part of me. You got to know a woman who was exhausted, frightened, and at the end of her rope. Why did you think that was all there was to me? I survived in those hills for six years. I saw my father shot to death before my eyes. I went through more than you can ever imagine." She stood up and tossed the garter belt aside. "You appear to think because I seem to have a gentle nature, that must denote some kind of weakness."

"I didn't say that, Samantha."

"But you believe it. You even told Skip to quit calling me Topaz." She came toward him, wearing only her jeweled slave bracelet and her topaz ring. "If I'm gentle, it's because I choose to be. Not because I'm incapable of being strong. I'm Samantha, but I'm also Topaz." She stopped by the bed. "I can't black out those six years because they helped to make me what I am. I'll always be both Samantha and Topaz for the rest of my life."

His eyes were hot as they ran over her, fastening on the tight, springy curls guarding her womanhood. "You can call yourself anything you want, if you'll just put some clothes on," he said thickly.

She shook her head. "Why?" Her gaze flicked down his body. "That's not what you want. You want me to come to bed with you, and that's what I'm going to do."

"No."

"Yes. We made a deal. You kept your part of it, now it's time for me to keep mine." She reached out and picked up his hand from the coverlet. A little shiver went through her; she had forgotten the blunt, sinewy power of that hand, and its warmth and hardness came as a sensual shock. She put his palm on the soft flesh of her belly and promptly felt a melting sensation between her thighs. "I'm going to have your baby, Fletch."

He snatched his hand away. "No."

She took a step nearer and placed her hand gently on the rough, springy auburn thatch pelting his chest. She felt a tremor, and then his chest contracted as if she had struck a brand to it. "I will," she whispered. "I told you I always keep my word." Her fingers trailed down his chest, feeling his muscles tense and harden in their path. "You want me. You want a child. I'll give you both. Anytime you want me." Her fingers curled in the coarse hair surrounding his manhood. "You can't stop it."

"I can." He spoke through gritted teeth, his jaw set as if she were torturing him. He shuddered as she sat down on the bed and rubbed her breasts against his chest. "Samantha...get away...from me."

She ignored him as she bent to lick delicately at the hollow of his shoulder. "You taste salty." She bit teasingly at his flesh. His chest was laboring as if he were running. "If you make me leave now, I'll only come back tomorrow. If you leave Paris, I'll follow you.

I'll make myself available in hotels, limousines, at your office. Shut me out and I'll still find a way to you, wherever you are." She brushed her nipples against him teasingly. "So why not give in now? It will save us both time and effort." She turned her face and licked lazily at his nipple. He made a sound that was between a gasp and a groan. "I think this is a good time for me. I'm not sure, but I believe I'm in a fertile period right now. You could put your seed in me and perhaps we—"

He broke.

"God!" He snatched her to him with bruising strength. One kiss, two, she lost count as his mouth drained her, took breath and power with dizzying strength. He was muttering words, but they were unintelligible, feverish, as he pulled her down over him. For an instant she was afraid; she could see none of the gentleness he had shown her the first time. He was all male lust.

He parted her thighs with frantic haste and sheathed her on his manhood. She bit her lower lip as waves of sensation shivered through her. Captured. Pinned. Unable to move except at his command. It was unbearably erotic. "Fletch..."

"Mine." His nostrils flared as he tried to force air into starved lungs. His hips bucked upward, forcing her to take more of him. "Mine, Samantha." His hands on her hips refused to let her give, only take. "This is... mine."

Possession. The most primitive, sensual possession she had ever imagined. She couldn't breathe. She threw back her head, and her lips parted as she struggled to survive through this heated belonging. "I think... you're..."

"You're *killing* me." His teeth were clenched. "So tight. It's like nothing..." He began to move. Gently at first, then harder, and finally wildly, deeply.

She clutched his shoulders, lost in a haze that was blindingly erotic.

"Give..." Fletch groaned.

She couldn't give any more; there was no

more to give. She tried, but the primitive rhythm was too intense. She could only hold on to the whirlwind, hold on to Fletch. Beauty. Wildness. Depth.

Then she was flung free of the whirlwind and at the same time clasped close to Fletch as spiraling passion exploded into a greater beauty than had gone before.

Her breasts were rising and falling as she tried to get her breath. "Dear heaven, Fletch," she whispered as she buried her face in his shoulder. "I never thought you'd react like that...." She trailed off; there weren't any words, anyway.

"Did I hurt you?" His voice was very low.

She laughed huskily. "Why are you always asking me that?"

"Well, did I?"

"No." Her lips brushed his shoulder. "Definitely not."

He lifted her off him. "I could have. I went crazy. You shouldn't have done that. I haven't had a woman for over four months."

"I liked it." She raised herself up on one elbow. "I *loved* it. I don't shatter when anyone puts a finger on me, you know."

"So you've been telling me." He turned over on his back, staring up at the midnight blue of the velvet canopy. "You still shouldn't have done this."

"Are you angry?"

He was silent for a moment. "No, but you shouldn't—"

"But I did do it," she said calmly. "And it wasn't easy. The role of vamp is pretty foreign to me."

He suddenly chuckled. "You could have fooled me. Circe couldn't have done a better job."

"That's not a kind comparison. I hear Circe was a most unpleasant lady. She turned men into swine."

"That's not so far off in this case. I sure behaved like a starving wolf."

"Oh, Fletch." She reached up and turned his face so that he was forced to meet her gaze. "Reassuring you every time we make love is going to become very tedious if you're not sensible and accept the fact that I enjoy what you do to me."

He went still. "You're speaking as if this is a permanent arrangement. You're still determined on this insanity?"

"I don't change my mind very readily."

He opened his lips and then closed them again without speaking. His gaze searched her face. "Were you telling me the truth about this being a fertile period?"

"It's entirely possible." She smiled. "But I think I'd better increase the odds. I'll come to you tomorrow night, and every night after that, until you leave. How long will you be in Paris?"

"I'm not sure," he said slowly.

"Then we'd better take advantage of the time we have." She slipped beneath the satin sheet, tucked the other side around Fletch, then curled up next to him like a friendly puppy. "Whenever you feel like it, we'll—" She yawned. "Oh, Lord, I'm sleepy again. Do you suppose this is going to happen all the time?" She made a face. "Some Circe. Just wake me up if you decide you want an encore."

His arm automatically went around her, cuddling her close. It was poignantly similar to that first night when she had fallen asleep in his arms. Similar, yet completely different. Now he was conscious of the steel beneath the softness, the strength that would bend but never break, Samantha and Topaz, one and the same.

After a long time he closed his eyes, his arms holding her with a possessiveness that still held an element of wariness. This was a mistake. He couldn't let her do this. Yet how could he stop her? His body responded to her as helplessly as if he had no will at all. He had never felt out of control in his life before, but he did now. He would have to steel himself.

She sighed and moved closer.

He smiled grimly in the darkness. Where was the steel now? Melted away as if it had never been by the touch of Samantha's nearness. Oh, well, he would worry about this unexpected development tomorrow. Meanwhile it was sweet to lie here and pretend that Samantha belonged to him. Very sweet.

He was sure his thoughts were of a radiant, gentle Samantha, but as he drifted off to sleep, the name he murmured was "Topaz."

Strength—warm, loving strength—entering her with exquisite gentleness. She was full. Brimming. The rhythm was starting again.

She opened drowsy eyes to look up at Fletch's face above her. "Lovely."

"Shhh, this won't be long, but I had to..." He stroked deep, his face drawn with a pleasure that was almost pain. "I tried not to do this. It's not..." A shudder rippled through him, the thrusting deepened. "But, Lord, I needed you."

Her arms slid around his shoulders, sleep

departing as desire arrived. "It's all right. You should have woke me sooner," she whispered. "I told you—"

His lips, covering her own, stopped the words. "Don't talk," he said when he lifted his head. "Just give to me. I need you to give to me. I don't want to take again."

There was something important, something she should think about in those tersely uttered words. But she couldn't think. Not now. She could only *feel*. Only instinct moved her, guided her. She began to undulate, helping him. "You never took." Searing pleasure peaked, burned, and then died to warm, glowing embers.

She was dimly aware of Fletch moving off her, then drawing her close once more. "I didn't mean to do that again," he said haltingly. "I'm sorry."

"I'm glad you did." Her lips drowsily caressed his arm. "It made me feel good, and it was nice not to be the aggressor for once."

"I think you must be mistaken." His voice

held a thread of humor. "I don't believe anyone has ever accused me of lack of aggressiveness before."

"Oh, I don't doubt you're a tiger in the
boardroom." She yawned. "Skip's always
telling me how intimidating you are."

"I obviously don't intimidate you. My
roars of protest certainly didn't stop you
earlier." His hand gently stroked her hair.
"My domain was attacked, invaded, and occupied before I knew what had happened."

She chuckled. "I believe I was the one who
was occupied."

There was silence in the room.

"Are you going to fight me on this?" she
asked quietly.

"Would it change your mind if I did?"

"No," she whispered. "But it would make
me less tense, if I knew I wasn't going to
have to seduce you every night. You might
just as well give in. I mean, I could already
be pregnant now. It would kind of be like
closing the barn door after the horses had
gone."

His hand moved to touch the soft smoothness of her belly. His warm palm rested there, unmoving, heavily possessive. "I won't fight you ... now."

He meant until he was sure there was no child, she thought with a pang. Well, a little victory was better than none at all. "Good." She closed her eyes. "I'm sure that will make things more pleasant for us both. Good night, Fletch. Sleep well."

"Sleep?" His hand slid lazily from her abdomen to between her thighs. His skilled fingers searched out and found their prize, then began flicking teasingly. "I have no intention of sleeping, Samantha."

A hot, aching shiver ran through her. "No?"

"Hell, no," he said softly. "It's been a long four months." Two fingers moved within her, and she had to bite her lip to keep from moaning with pleasure. "Do you know how many nights I lay awake and thought about that night in the cave? You won't have to worry about seducing me. It's more likely you'll have to think of ways to discourage me." He drew the sheet back and came over her, gently nudging her womanhood. "Is this aggressive enough for you, love? Is this what you want?"

Nothing could be more aggressive than Fletch as he crouched over her, all male sexuality and sensual dominance. Strong thighs; tense, massive chest moving in and out with the harshness of his breathing; nostrils flaring in a face taut with desire. Just looking at him caused heat between her thighs.

"Yes, Fletch." Her legs encircled his hips, welcoming him into her. "That's what I want."

"Where the devil are you going?" Fletch raised up on one elbow to frown at Samantha across the room. "Come back to bed."

She shook her head as she wriggled into the golden gown. "I have a class at nine."

She came back to bed and turned around. "Will you help me with this zipper?"

"I take it the seduction is over?" He jerked the zipper up with a force that caused a hissed screaming of metal on metal. "I wouldn't want to interfere with something really important."

"It *is* important," she said calmly. "And there's no reason why I should miss it when you'll probably be involved with your business meetings today, anyway."

He was silent, scowling at her. "I could cancel my meetings."

"Nonsense." She walked across the room to where she had slipped off her sandals the night before. "Our agreement was that I wasn't to interfere with your professional life. It's very kind of you to try to make me feel I'm not imposing on you, but—"

"You're not imposing."

She slipped on her sandals. "Will you call your chauffeur? I'm almost ready." She ran her fingers through her tousled hair. "I don't think I'm really suited for one-night stands. I feel terribly ... mussed."

She was actually leaving him, Fletch realized with indignation and an odd sense of panic. He was not going to be able to convince her not to go. Not that he'd actually asked her to stay, but he *had* offered to cancel his meetings, dammit. "I ... I want you to stay."

"That's nice to know." She lifted her head and smiled at him. "Then you'll be glad to see me when I come back tonight." She turned and walked toward the door. "Tell Pierre I'll be waiting at the front door."

He sat up in bed. "What time will you be here tonight?"

"Late." She glanced over her shoulder as she opened the door. "I have an evening class too. I'll call Skip and ask him to pick me up when I'm sure I'll be free."

"That's very good of you." The irony in his tone was lost on Samantha, for she had closed the door behind her.

He gazed moodily at the telephone on the

bedside table. He was tempted not to call Pierre at the gate house but to go after Samantha and bring her back to his bed. He wanted her again. His body was as ready for her as if they hadn't made love innumerable times in the last hours. Damn, he had never felt like this before. He was in a fever for her. He couldn't get enough.

He slowly reached out his hand and picked up the receiver, punching in the number of the gate house. To give in to a fever this strong would be madness. He would fight it, subdue this passion as he had subdued lesser passions, since experience had taught him how dangerous uncontrolled emotion can be. He would let her go and prove to himself that Samantha could not dominate his body as she did his thoughts.

Pierre picked up his phone, and Fletch spoke briskly to him, then hung up abruptly.

Besides, he told himself, she had promised to come back that night.

"I want you to move into the château." Fletch's lips brushed her temple. "It's sheer stupidity for you to have to be driven back and forth in the wee hours every night."

"I don't mind the ride. It gives me time to think."

"Well, I mind. For the last six nights you haven't gotten here until after midnight, and you leave before daybreak. This commuting is getting too much for you. You look tired."

She laughed as she cuddled closer. "So do you. I usually manage time for a short nap in the afternoon. I'd wager you drive yourself all day. Right?"

"My schedule is pretty tight."

"Maybe I should stay home a few nights so that you can get some rest."

His arms tightened instantly around her. "No."

"It would probably be the sensible thing—"

His lips covered hers with desperate force. "Shut up," he muttered. "The sensible thing for you to do is to move in here where we can spread our lovemaking over a twenty-four-hour period."

"And you think we'd do that?"

He kissed her again. "No, I'd probably want you every minute you were here. I'd take you in the halls, on the terrace..." He kissed her again. "In the scullery."

"It sounds kinky." Her voice was breathless. "Particularly the scullery."

"Then you'll move in?"

She shook her head. "I have no place here."

"The hell you haven't. You're my wife."

"Am I?" She smiled sadly. "I don't feel at all married. Perhaps after I become pregnant I'll come to live here until the baby is born. It would probably be healthier living in the country."

"And after the baby is born?"

"I don't know," she said quietly. "Things have changed. I'm taking one step at a time."

He was silent, and she could feel the tension stiffening his body. "You said you didn't think you'd be able to leave your child."

"I know." She closed her eyes. "I don't want to talk about it at the moment, Fletch."

"What harm would it do for you to move in with me now?"

Her eyes opened, and she shook her head in rueful amusement. "Good heavens but you're persistent."

"I want you here."

"We can't always have what we want. Even the great Fletcher Bronson. You'll have to be contented with our midnight rendezvous."

His voice was muffled as he buried his lips in the hair at her temple. "That's sex, and it's not only sex I want, blast it. I want to *see* you. Lately I've been remembering that morning in the cave when I brought you the melon and watched you eat it. I want to have breakfast with you, *talk* to you."

Surely that meant they were becoming closer. Samantha quickly masked the ripple of hope she was experiencing. "How romantic," she said lightly. "But if I remember correctly, you scowled at me all through that momentous meal and nagged me until I wanted to strangle you."

"You didn't eat enough."

"I think we'll both be happier with the present arrangement. Sans breakfast."

"You're a very stubborn woman. I guess I'll just have to fit in with your guidelines for coming to live with me."

"What do you mean?"

He moved over her, his gaze holding hers as he slowly slid into her body. "The child. I'll just have to redouble my efforts to make you pregnant."

She laughed shakily. "That would be an impossibility. There are limits."

"No," he muttered as he began to move faster, harder. "Not with you, Samantha. Not with you, love."

Where the devil was she?

It was nearly three in the morning and she wasn't here yet.

His hand clenched on the sheet. He *wanted* her. What kind of game was she playing with him? First letting him become accustomed to her presence in his bed, and then not showing up when he needed her.

It wasn't until four that he admitted she might not come.

He would *not* go to her. He wouldn't admit to the need that had become an insatiable craving. If she didn't want him, he would find another woman. Monette was filming in the wine country only a short flight away. He would send for her and let her take away—

But he didn't want Monette. He didn't want anyone but Samantha.

It would pass. It had to pass. He reached over and turned out the light.

But he was still lying awake, staring into the darkness, when the first tentative rays of the sun whispered softly into the room.

Waiting. She would come. He couldn't have been mistaken in the passion she had shown him. He knew she would come.

But she didn't come that night.

And she didn't come the next night.

Nor the night after that.

The knocking was so loud, it sounded like separate explosions, jarring Samantha from her uneasy sleep.

"Samantha, dammit, let me in."

Fletch!

She threw back the covers and jumped from the daybed. Oh, Lord, she had been half expecting that knock for the last four days, but it still came as a shock.

"Samantha, open the door."

"Hush, stop shouting. I'm coming." She slipped on her robe as she hurried to the door. "You'll wake up everyone in the *pension*." She unfastened the chain lock and threw open the door. "It's two o'clock in the morning, for heaven's sake. Couldn't you—" She stopped, inhaling sharply as she looked into his face. His light eyes were glittering wildly, and the tension surrounding him was nearly tangible.

"I know what time it is." He pushed by her and slammed the door. "And I know what day it is. Thursday. That's four days, Samantha. *Four* days."

"Fletch, let me tell you—"

"Not now, you can talk to me later," he muttered. "You can bet I'm going to make sure you talk to me later in some detail. But not now." He pulled her close, shutting his eyes as he rubbed her yearningly against him. "This is what I want now. What I've got to have." He dropped down into the easy chair beside the door and pulled her down on his lap. One trembling palm ran over her breasts, impatiently pushing down the straps of the nightgown to get to her. "Do you want me?" His raw demand was harshly erotic as his bold arousal pressed against her.

His warm, hard palm caressing her breast

brought a wild thrill in its wake. Did she *want* him? She had tossed and turned on the daybed, aching, throbbing for him for four nights that had seemed like forever. She was as wild for their joining as he was. "Yes," she whispered. "Oh, yes."

It was all he needed. He quickly freed himself, swung her around to straddle him, and sheathed himself in her with one strong stroke.

He groaned, burying his lips in the hollow of her throat. "Tell me if I hurt you. I'm a little crazy tonight." He began to move. There was violence but no pain. Burning but no destruction. It was insanity. It was hunger and a frantic need. It was too much. She didn't know when the tears began to run down her cheeks. She wasn't aware of anything but Fletch within her.

It was too wild to last for very long, their passion too intense not to explode with a force that left them both weak, clinging desperately to each other in the aftermath.

Fletch lifted his head from her neck, but

he lifted it, slowly, jerkily, as if it were heavily weighted. "I thought I wanted to strangle you when I left the château tonight." His voice was just a level above a hoarse whisper. "But I was lying to myself. This was what I wanted. No matter how angry I was with you, I guess I knew all I wanted was to have you with me like this."

"You were angry with me?"

He looked at her in blank surprise. "You're damn right I was angry with you." Anger flared again in his eyes as he lifted her off him and adjusted his clothing and then her own. "I'm still angry. Why shouldn't I be?"

"Because I didn't do anything to make you angry."

"You didn't come to me, you didn't phone me. If I hadn't had Skip check on you, I wouldn't have known if you'd had an accident or were ill or—"

She tightened the belt of her robe. "I'm not ill."

"Is that all you have to say?" His eyes

blazed down at her. "Why didn't you come to me?"

"I've been busy."

"Why, Samantha?"

She gave in. "It was getting too difficult for me. You're a little overpowering, Fletch. I wasn't expecting it to be this...this all-consuming. Every night it got a little worse." She shrugged wearily. "I thought it would be best to give us both some breathing room."

"It doesn't work like that, Samantha. You can't take five steps forward and one step back. You're the one who initiated this course of events." His lips twisted. "Did you ever initiate! I was so set on being self-sacrificing that I could have earned a halo, but you wouldn't have it. You came to me and tied me up in knots. And now I can't think of anything at all but you and what we do together."

"I can't think of anything else, either, and it scares me," she said simply. "I'm getting terribly involved."

"Involved? How did you expect not to get involved if you made love to me?"

Her lips were trembling as she tried to smile. "You didn't become involved with Miss Santore."

"That was different—you're different." He drew a deep breath. "*We're* different."

Samantha gazed at him with a faint stirring of hope. "Are we?"

"Of course we are. Do you think I'd chase anyone but you to this hovel at the top of the world?" He frowned. "And that's another thing: Why the devil are you in this dump, anyway? I told Pierre he was crazy when he stopped in front of the *pension*, until I realized I'd better check the names on the mailboxes. I've learned from experience that you're capable of almost any madness."

"This isn't a dump, it's my home. I like it."

"You prefer a shabby one-room studio to a château? You have very peculiar tastes."

"I suppose you're right." She turned away.

"However, I do have a hot plate. Would you like a cup of coffee?"

"No, I don't want coffee. I want to know why you wouldn't move into the château when you first came here to Paris. I wasn't on the scene, so it couldn't have been a distaste for my company."

"I don't have a distaste for your company."

"Not in bed."

"Not anytime. It's just..." She made a helpless gesture with her hand. "I didn't have the right to take anything from you if I wasn't giving you anything in return. I thought that would change, but when I found out you had lied to me about our agreement—"

"You decided to take matters into your own hands," Fletch said wearily. "But you still won't move in with me. I can't take much more of this, Samantha."

She dropped down on the daybed and clasped her hands tightly together. "It's exactly what you said you wanted," she whispered. "I don't bother you. You can devote yourself entirely to your business interests. I give you sex now and I'll give you a child later. It's the perfect situation for you."

"You don't bother me?" he repeated incredulously. "You're driving me crazy."

Her gaze dropped to her clenched hands. "I never meant to disrupt your life. Once we're sure the child is conceived, I'll go away if you like."

"No!" he said sharply. He dropped to his knees in front of her and gathered her hands in his own. "You're not going anywhere. You're going to stay with me."

"But you said—"

"I said you drive me crazy, and you do." He lifted her chin and forced her to meet his eyes. "Because it's too much and yet not enough. I want you to come home with me, Samantha," he said softly. "I don't know if I can maintain even a halfway normal relationship, but I want to try. I want to have you near me."

"Why?"

He hesitated. "Because I think we have a chance for something pretty special to happen between us." He grimaced. "Maybe not as special for you as for me. That was why I tried to push you away before you came too close. But you're a very determined young lady, you just kept coming."

Samantha felt as if the breath had been knocked out of her, and joy began to spiral through her in glittering waves. "More than sex? More than the child? You think maybe we can..."

He nodded. "I know I'm not every woman's idea of a romantic hero, and I've got quite a few years on you, but we could try."

Her eyes were glittering with tears. "Oh, yes, we could try." Her hand tightened on his. "I think that would be a wonderful idea."

His breath came out in a little rush and he smiled at her. He jumped to his feet. "It's settled, then. Come on, let's go. I'll help you pack."

Astonished, she stared at him. "You want me to move in the middle of the night?"

He pulled her to her feet. "We'll pack just enough of your clothes to last until we can buy you some more, and I'll send someone to pick up the rest of your things. I gather that gold gown was a onetime splurge?"

"Yes, I didn't want—"

He silenced her with a quick, hard kiss. "But everything's changed now, right? It's a new slate."

A new slate. She only hoped they could inscribe something on it that would last a lifetime. She nodded happily. "Right."

He turned away. "Where's your luggage? I'll start packing while you dress."

A tiny smile tugged at her lips. Fletch was throwing himself into the project with characteristic energy. "My suitcase is in the closet." She went to the bureau and pulled out jeans, underthings, and a sweatshirt, then grabbed her tennis shoes from behind the screen. She turned to the door. "I'll be right back. The bathroom is down the hall."

"You don't have a private bathroom?" His lips tightened. "Samantha, why couldn't you at least have rented a place—" He stopped and shook his head. "A new slate is definitely required. I can hardly wait until I get you home and organize you."

"I'm not a bankrupt company," she told him serenely. "And you'll organize me only as much as I choose to let you."

His laughter held a note of surprise. "Point taken...Topaz."

When she returned ten minutes later, he had removed the damp cloth from the statue she was working on and was standing there gazing at it.

"I'm flattered," he said gruffly as he heard the door close behind him. "Not that you could do anything to make me look as pretty as your friend, Ricardo, but you at least re-membered what I looked like."

"No, you're not pretty." She moved for-ward to stand beside him. "But you have a face that will endure and still be this strong and riveting when all the pretty faces are forgotten." She reached up and gently touched the cheek of the statue. "Not many faces reflect what's inside a person, but yours does, Fletch. It's honest and bold and intelligent." Her index finger touched the corner of the statue's lips. "And there are lines of humor here."

"Is that how you see me?"

She nodded, feeling suddenly shy. She hurriedly looked at the bed and to the open suitcase in which a wild variety of clothes had been heaped. "You call that packing?"

He nodded absently, his gaze still on the statue.

She crossed the room and quickly straightened the clothing in the suitcase before shutting and fastening it. "Heaven help me if this is an example of your 'organization.' "

"I was in a hurry. I always save my energy for the more important projects. You qualify first on that list." He slowly put the cloth back over the statue. "Thank you."

"For immortalizing you?" she asked lightly.

He shook his head. "For seeing me with ... kindness." He abruptly turned away, strode across the room, and picked up the suitcase from the bed. "Let's get out of here." He took her elbow and propelled her toward the door. "I want to get you home."

"Fletch ..." Her voice was hesitant. "How do you see me?"

"With—" He stopped, and something dark, wild, and yet undeniably tender flitted across his face. He opened the door. "I see you as an obsession. My own very special obsession."

NINE

"COME ON, SAMANTHA!" Fletch burst into her studio with his usual explosiveness. He grabbed her hand and pulled her away from the statue she was working on and toward the door. "You can do that later."

"But I want to finish the last bit." She began to laugh helplessly as she was half led, half pulled out of the studio and down the hall. "May I ask where we're going?"

"Dinner?"

"Dinner was three hours ago," she said dryly. "As I recall, you spent it closeted in your office in the city with Señor Rivera and those other mysterious gentlemen from Spain."

"They're not mysterious. I know exactly who they are and how they think," Fletch muttered. "Greedy bastards." He cast her a scowling glance. "And you should have eaten without me instead of going back to your studio to work. When I spoke to Skip on the phone, he said you hadn't had anything to eat since lunch, and it's nearly ten now."

"I had a sandwich." She frowned, trying to remember. "I think."

"You didn't," he said flatly. "Not a bite." He hustled her down the grand staircase. "But we'll take care of that right now."

Her lips quirked. "Yes, master. Whatever you decree. May I at least wash my hands first?"

"No." He pulled a spotless white handkerchief from his pocket and handed it to her. "Wipe them on this."

She began to dab at the clay on her palms.

"Fletch, you're being ridiculous. A few more minutes won't matter."

"Yes, it will." His grin was almost boyish. "I can't wait."

She gazed at him in puzzlement. "You're that hungry?"

He shook his head as he pushed her through the library toward the French doors leading to the terrace. "You'll see." He threw open the French doors and stepped aside to let her precede him.

Cool moonlight vied with the warmth of the flickering flames of tall candles to cast an aura of intimate enchantment on the gleaming crystal, fine china, and white orchid centerpiece on the damask-covered table. The wild, sweet strains of Gypsy violins drifted faintly to them from the gazebo in the center of the formal garden.

Dazzled, Samantha stopped, gazing at the scene. "Are we having a party?"

"Dinner." Fletch's gaze was fixed eagerly on her face, drinking in her reaction. "I ordered the duck à l'orange from Maxim's."

"I didn't realize they had take-out service." Her glance shifted to the gazebo. "Did you order the Gypsies too?"

"I thought it appropriate." He walked over to the table and pulled back her chair. "They wanted to serenade us here on the terrace, but I hate to have musicians hovering around dipping their bows in my soup, so I stuck them in the gazebo." He frowned uncertainly. "Would you rather have them here? I could tell them to come running."

"No, they're fine in the gazebo." She sat down, trying to smother the laughter that threatened to escape. The image of Fletch snapping his fingers and the entire troupe of musicians bolting across the garden suddenly made her want to giggle like a schoolgirl. "It would probably spoil the mood."

Fletch nodded as he seated himself opposite her. "Do you like them?" he asked. "Is everything all right?"

"Wonderful." She breathed in the scented air. "I had no idea you could be so romantic."

"I'm not romantic." He unfolded the napkin and spread it on his lap. "I just thought you might like this. I've heard women have a thing for Gypsy violins and candlelight." He vaguely waved his hand to encompass the entire scene. "And all this."

"We do." She leaned back in her chair, her gaze wandering dreamily over the garden. "Or at least I do. Thank you, Fletch."

"You can thank me by eating your dinner," he said gruffly. "You're really pleased?"

Her gaze moved from the garden to rest on Fletch's face. Why, he actually appeared anxious. She had never seen him this unsure, and it both stirred and touched her. "You couldn't have done anything that pleased me more." She wrinkled her nose at him. "Except pick a night when I wasn't wearing jeans and a stained T-shirt. I would like to have dressed up for the occasion."

He shook his head. "It had to be tonight. I had to show you—" He broke off and reached for the bottle of champagne in the ice bucket on the cart beside the table. "You look fine. You always look great."

"What did you have to show me?"

He poured the champagne into her glass. "I had to show you that it's worth it," he said gravely. "That no matter how much I seem to neglect you, I'll always make up for it later. I'll never undervalue our relationship, and I'll never take you for granted." He set the bottle back into the bucket. "That meeting tonight really was important, Samantha. I wouldn't have—"

"Wait just a minute. You arranged a deluxe meal from Maxim's, champagne, orchids, and Gypsy violinists just to say you were sorry you were late for dinner?"

"I suppose you think it's a guilt trip?" A frown wrinkled his brow. "I guess in a way it is, but it's not as if this happens all the time. It's the first evening I haven't been home for dinner since you moved into the château three weeks ago. We've spent every evening together, and I've tried to be home for lunch. It's not as if I've been neglecting you—Why are you laughing?"

"I'm sorry." Her eyes were dancing. "I was just thinking that only you would go to these extremes to make amends for an incident most husbands wouldn't even bother to acknowledge."

"But I'm not most husbands, and this isn't most marriages. I'm not used to doing a juggling act between my business and my personal life, so I have to work harder."

Her smile faded. "You have been working hard at it," she said gently. "But I wasn't aware you were worrying like this. You shouldn't have been so foolish."

"I wasn't worrying, I was just—" He stopped, a rueful smile curving his lips. "I'm lying. I was gnawing my nails to the quick, imagining you packing your bags and bolting when I couldn't get away from Rivera tonight." He met her gaze. "I like what we've got together, Samantha. I don't want to blow it."

Samantha experienced a wild surge of

happiness, and she had to swallow to ease the sudden tightness in her throat. "Neither do I."

He went still. "You mean that? You think it's working?"

"Fletch, we have terrific sex, and we enjoy all the other times together too. Why shouldn't I think it's working?"

"How do I know what you're thinking? You never tell me." He gestured impatiently to keep her from speaking. "Oh, I know you like what I do to you in bed, but that's not enough for me. I want more. I want to know you...." He trailed off, and she saw his hand clench into a fist on the table. "You don't seem very worried about me neglecting you. Maybe you'd prefer that I don't come home to dinner every evening."

She burst out laughing. "First you're worried that I will mind, and now you're worried that I won't. You're not being very reasonable."

"I don't feel reasonable. Do you want me to come home to dinner or not?"

Her smile vanished as she gazed at him. He was serious. She reached out to cover his clenched fist with her hand. "I want you to come home and be with me as much as you're able to," she said softly. "However, I'm trying to be very mature and sensible about this. I know you love your work, as I love mine, and I realize there'll be times when we can't be together."

"But you *were* disappointed when I didn't come home tonight?"

She had to hide another smile. He was like a small boy pleading for reassurance of his importance in the scheme of things. "Very disappointed," she told him solemnly.

His rare smile lit his harsh features with warmth. "I'll try not to do it again."

Tenderness flowed through her. "See that you do. Next time I'll be very fierce with you if you're even one minute late."

His hand turned over to capture hers. "I'll remember." His clasp tightened. "It really is working, isn't it, Samantha?"

She gazed at Fletch in the moonlight, loving him. Little boy, ruthless aggressor, passionate lover—he was all these things and more. So much more. Sometimes it was actually painful to restrain herself from telling him all he meant to her, and this was one of those moments.

But soon she would be able to tell him. They were growing closer all the time, and his reaction tonight filled her with hope as well as joy. Any day now he would say the words she yearned to hear. Any day now...

"How could it not work?" she said lightly. "When you ply a woman with Gypsy violins and dinner from Maxim's?"

There was something very satisfying about gardening, Samantha thought contentedly as she planted the last fragile slip the gardener had reluctantly relinquished from his jealous charge. In a way it gave her a creative fulfillment similar to the one she experienced when sculpting, yet was far more relaxing. The pressure of total control and responsibility was absent here. Plants required sun and rain and nutrients to—

"Lord, you're solemn, Topaz. Have you just buried your pet parakeet or something?"

She glanced up to see Skip grinning down at her and made a face at him. "I'm thinking deep thoughts. You ought to try it sometime."

He shuddered theatrically. "The mere idea appalls me. I prefer to coast along on the surface of life. I've always found it to be a much smoother ride. Why are you groveling in the dirt? I couldn't believe it when I couldn't find you in your studio."

"I don't work all the time." And she hadn't felt like detracting from the night before by involving herself in her work. She had wanted to savor all the nuances of what had happened on that moonlit terrace. Savor, and perhaps daydream a little about what could be just beyond the horizon. "I thought I'd take a break today."

"So you immediately proceed to labor in the garden instead of your studio. I feel it my duty to give you a few instructions in the fine art of taking a break. I'm a world-class expert at it."

She laughed. "Maybe you should start with Fletch first; he's a much more advanced case. Is that why you were looking for me?"

"Nope, there's someone to see you, Topaz. He's waiting in the study."

Samantha took off her gardening gloves and wiped the perspiration from her forehead with the sleeve of her blouse. "To see me? I don't know anyone in Paris except the students at school, and the château is too far for one of them to just casually drop in. It's probably someone trying to hit up Fletch Bronson's wife for a donation. Why don't you tend to it, Skip?"

He shook his head. "I think you'd better see him. It's an old friend of yours, and he's come a long way."

"An old friend?" Her eyes lit with excitement. "Who is it?"

"Ricardo Lazaro. I just picked him up at the airport."

"But what's Ricardo doing here in France?" She hurriedly got to her feet. "The last I heard from him he was still in Barbados."

"When was that?"

"A few weeks after I arrived here in Paris from Damon's Reef." Samantha started quickly down the path toward the terrace. "Why didn't he let me know he was coming?"

"He probably didn't know himself." Skip fell into step with her. "Fletch didn't decide he needed him until last night, after his meeting with Rivera. He told me to arrange to have him flown in double quick."

"*Need* him? Why should Fletch need Ricardo to help with one of his business deals?"

"I have no idea. I just do what the man says. Maybe you should ask Lazaro."

"I will." She hesitated as she reached the French doors. She was hot and sweaty, and her blue-jean shorts were less than clean. Oh, well, Ricardo had seen her looking a great deal worse over the years, and she couldn't wait to see him. "You said he's in the study?"

Skip nodded. "I had orders to bring him to Fletch's office in town, but Lazaro insisted I bring him to see you first. Don't keep him too long, okay? Fletch isn't going to like having his arrangements shot down." He dropped into a cushioned lounge chair, pulled the bill of his cap down over his eyes, and lazily stretched his legs out before him. "I believe I'll sit here and catch a few rays. Call me when you finish."

Samantha nodded absently as she entered the house.

Ricardo looked wonderfully fit, magnificently good-looking, and so elegant in his biscuit-colored business suit that she was momentarily intimidated. Then he smiled and she felt immediately at ease. Ricardo would never change. Perhaps on the surface there would be alterations, but he would still remain what he had always been; a friend who was closer than any brother could be.

His dark face was suddenly illuminated by a flashing white smile. "*Querida,* I hoped for better things of the grand Mrs. Bronson. Here I was expecting to see you in a Dior dress and fine Italian shoes, and what do I find? Bare feet, blue-jean shorts, and dirty knees. You're a great disappointment to me." He held out his arms. "But I will make the great sacrifice and hug you, anyway."

She flew across the room and hurled herself into his arms. "Ricardo." Her arms tightened around him. "You're well? Your wound?"

"I'm completely well." His lips brushed her forehead. "And you, Samantha?"

"Getting fat." She drew back to look into his face. "And very happy to see you. Have you seen Paco?"

He nodded. "He's still in Bridgetown waiting for me to get back with the final word from Bronson."

Her brow knitted in bewilderment. "What word?"

Richardo's eyes narrowed. "You don't know?"

"Evidently I don't. What is there to know?"

He shrugged. "I thought he would have told you. But perhaps not. He's a difficult man to try to anticipate."

"Ricardo, what on earth are you talking about? And why did Fletch have you flown here from Barbados without telling me?"

"The Rivera faction is giving him problems. He thought I might be able to tip the balance his way." He pulled a face. "He says he needs my image. I think he means to *promote* me."

"Ricardo." She released her breath with exasperation. "Tell me, blast it. What's happening?"

"The revolution," he said simply. "The same lyrics but a different melody, brilliantly orchestrated by one Fletcher Bronson."

"What?" she asked faintly. Her knees felt

suddenly weak, and she took a step back to half lean, half sit against the Sheraton desk. "The revolution is over. We were beaten."

"That's what I thought." Ricardo's ebony eyes were suddenly glowing in his bronze face. "Until Bronson contacted me when I was in the hospital in Barbados. I couldn't believe it. It was a miracle."

"Fletch is very good at performing miracles," she murmured. "But this one would have to be on a grand scale."

"I don't think he knows how to operate on any other level," Ricardo said dryly. "He informed me that I had bungled the entire revolution, but he thought he could put it right if I placed myself in his hands."

"That sounds like Fletch. Are you going to do it?"

"I already have. Why do you think I'm here? Fletcher says that a revolution, like everything else, takes two things: money and clout. For the past five months he's been wheeling and dealing on both sides of the Atlantic to acquire enormous reserves of both. According to him, all I have to supply is my humble self as the figurehead and he'll do the rest." He slowly shook his head. "Your husband is quite a man, *querida*."

"Yes, I know." Her head was whirling. Why had Fletch done this? And why hadn't he told her?

"Did he tell you why—" She stopped. Ricardo was shaking his head. "Nothing?"

"I thought you might have converted him to the cause." He shrugged. "That refinery he owns on St. Pierre certainly wouldn't be worth all this effort."

"I've never discussed St. Pierre with him."

"Then I'm as much in the dark as you are." Ricardo frowned. "And I don't like to be uncertain of the motives of a man like Fletcher Bronson. There's too much at stake. Can I trust him, Samantha?"

"Yes," she answered unequivocally.

His face cleared and he smiled gently. "That's good. I'm glad you have such faith in him. I was very worried when you wrote me about your marriage. I thought you'd rushed into it too quickly after leaving St. Pierre. So many things could have driven you to him. Fear, exhaustion, uncertainty about the future..." He took a step forward and touched her cheek with his index finger. "But there is love, *querida*?"

"There is love," she answered softly. "So much love."

"Ah, now I feel better." He kissed her lightly on the tip of the nose. "About my friend and about my revolution. You have always had impeccable judgment in men, or you would not hold me in such affection." He stepped back. "And now I'd better have the good Mr. Brennen take me back to Paris to see your husband. One mustn't irritate one's benefactors." He grinned impishly. "You see how wonderfully diplomatic I'm becoming? Bronson would be proud of his figurehead."

"Knowing you, it won't last. But I'll be proud of you whether you're diplomatic or not. You have a meeting with Rivera today?"

He shook his head. "Not until tomorrow.

I was just paying a courtesy call to Bronson before going to my hotel."

"Hotel? But you'll stay here, of course."

He shook his head. "I'm staying at the InterContinental. Bronson says that will be more convenient for the meeting with Rivera."

"Perhaps it would be more practical," she said doubtfully. "But I still wish..." Her face brightened. "Well, if I can't have you here, I'll steal you away for a little while now. You can see Fletch later. I want to show you my atelier and introduce you to Monsieur Dalbert, my teacher. Then we'll see a few sights together. Stay here, I'll be right back, as soon as I shower and change." She turned toward the door. "Ring if you'd like a drink."

"Samantha, I should really go to your husband's office first."

She hesitated as she opened the door. He was probably right. Fletch was never pleased about having his plans disrupted, but she wanted this time with Ricardo. Not only because she cared about him but also because he would be a bulwark to keep her from thinking about this secrecy of Fletch's. She would be a nervous wreck if she had to wait until Fletch came home that evening to get to the bottom of this business. She looked over her shoulder at Ricardo. "I'll tell Skip to call him and tell him I've kidnapped you." Her eyes twinkled. "Don't worry, I won't endanger your revolution. What could a few hours matter?"

He shook his head with an indulgent smile. "None, I suppose. I hope you're planning on taking me somewhere outrageously expensive, as befits your consequence. I'll enjoy watching our little Topaz play the grande dame."

She made a face. "If it will amuse you, I'll try. Though I have an idea I'll make an awful fool of myself. There are more pitfalls on this terrain than there were in the rain forests, Ricardo."

"And you'll learn to avoid them just as

you did the ones on St. Pierre." He smiled. "Fletcher Bronson is an excellent guide."

Her face lit with tenderness. "Yes," she whispered. "Yes, he is." She turned. "I promise I won't be more than fifteen minutes."

The door closed softly behind her.

TEN

THE FRONT DOOR slammed with an explosive crash. "Skip!"

Skip flinched and braced himself before rising from the easy chair and moving reluctantly toward the door leading to the foyer. He might as well get it over with, he thought gloomily. He had been expecting Fletch since he had heard the phone disconnect over an hour ago. It would do no good to try to avoid the confrontation. "Here, Fletch."

Fletch strode into the study and slammed that door too. "Is she back yet?"

"She left only an hour and a half ago." Skip tried to make his tone soothing. He might just as well have tried to pour a cup of water on an erupting Mt. Vesuvius.

"She wouldn't have left at all if you'd done what you were supposed to do." Fletch crossed the room and poured himself a whiskey at the portable bar. "Who the hell told you to bring Lazaro here?"

"He did. He wanted to see Topaz."

Fletch's hand tightened on the glass. "Her name is Samantha, and I didn't bring him across the ocean to see my wife."

"For Pete's sake, Fletch, what difference does it make? He would have seen her sometime before he left Paris."

"Not if you hadn't interfered. She wouldn't even have known he was here."

Skip blinked. "You didn't intend to tell her Lazaro was in Paris?"

"You're damn right I didn't." Fletch finished his drink in two swallows and poured himself another. "Not yet."

Skip shook his head. "That doesn't

make sense. They're very close friends. You couldn't have kept them apart if they were in the same city. How did you think you could pull it off?"

"A whirlwind flurry of conferences and an equally fast dash to the airport for him." Fletch turned away from the bar and threw himself into the wing chair by the desk. "I would have managed if you hadn't acted on your own and brought him here."

"I didn't know you considered it important to keep them apart," Skip said quietly. "And I still don't see why you're so upset about Top—Samantha renewing her acquaintance with Lazaro."

"Because I knew she—" Fletch broke off. "Take my word for it, you made a mistake. A big mistake."

"Then I'm sorry. Is there anything I can do to make amends?" One corner of Skip's lips lifted in a lopsided grin. "I could hop in the car and see if I could find them."

"In a city the size of Paris?" Fletch wearily shook his head. "No way. Besides, the harm is done now. I'll just have to wait and see how the chips fall. Did she say when she'd be back?"

"She expected to be out for the rest of the day." Skip's expression was troubled as he gazed at Fletch's face. He had never seen him like this. He had expected anger but not this sharp edge of desperation. "Fletch..."

Fletch closed his eyes, leaning his head back against the cushioned headrest. "It's okay, Skip. Maybe you did the right thing. Who the hell knows?"

"Listen, I don't know what you're worried about," Skip said hesitantly. "But Samantha is pretty special. You can trust her."

"I know I can trust her."

"Then why are you worried?"

"I'm not worried." Fletch's lids lifted, and a shock ran through Skip at what he saw there. "I'm scared to death."

"Fletch, I'm home. Are you here?"

Samantha closed the front door and tossed her purse on the chair by the door. Lord, she wanted Fletch to be home. A strange excitement had been growing within her all afternoon. All the time she had been with Ricardo she had been conscious of it but had resolutely ignored it. It was almost as if she had been afraid to acknowledge that there might be a reason for its existence. That there might be the possibility that the time had—

"Have you had dinner?" Fletch was standing in the doorway of the study, gazing at her with a blank expression. She experienced a sinking disappointment until she noticed the leashed tension that corded every muscle in his large body.

She nodded. "I dropped Ricardo off at his hotel and we ate in one of the hotel dining rooms." She smiled. "This time I'm the one who didn't come home in time for dinner. Perhaps I should have brought *you* Gypsy violinists and champagne from Maxim's."

"I'm not in the mood for Gypsy violinists, I'm afraid." His gaze was narrowed on her face. "I guess you and Lazaro had time to talk over old times. You were gone all afternoon."

She nodded as she walked toward him. "Yes, we did."

His eyes became wary. "And did you talk about the future too?"

"A little." She stopped before him. "Why didn't you tell me what you and Ricardo were planning?"

"Because I didn't want you to know," he said curtly. "And you wouldn't have known if Skip hadn't pulled the blunder of the century. You wouldn't even have been aware that Lazaro was in Paris."

Her eyes widened. "You wouldn't have told me?"

"No way."

"But why?" She laughed uncertainly. "It's not reasonable to—"

"That's what Skip said," he replied, interrupting. "Of course, it's not reasonable.

When have I ever been reasonable where you were concerned? I didn't want you to see Lazaro, dammit."

A tiny burst of happiness unfolded within her. "Why? You couldn't possibly have been jealous?"

"It wasn't jealousy." He scowled. "Well, not altogether. I can't say I like you spending time with a man who's as good-looking as Tom Cruise. I guess I'm pretty territorial."

"You are?" Her voice was breathless, the excitement expanding, growing in leaps and bounds. "But you know Ricardo is only my friend."

"That doesn't help much when I look in the mirror and compare his face with this rough mug of mine." He shrugged. "But I can face that kind of competition. I trust you, and besides, I'm not about to let any man take you away from me now. I'd find some way of getting rid of him."

The brutal flatness of the words sent a shiver through her. "Then why weren't you going to tell me that Ricardo was here?"

"It wasn't Lazaro that scared me; it was St. Pierre. You're not going back there, Samantha." His gaze was fixed on her face with compelling power. "When Lazaro returns to the island to launch the revolution, you're not going to be with him. Do you hear me? I won't have it."

"If you feel that strongly about it, why did you become involved in trying to breathe life into Ricardo's cause?"

"It's certainly not because I'm a bloody idealist like Lazaro," he said quickly. "Those blasted Marxists stole my refinery."

The beginning of a smile touched her lips. "I don't think that's the reason. Even an idealist like Ricardo realized that the refinery wasn't worth your launching another revolution to reclaim it."

"Did he? Maybe he has more common sense than I thought."

"He's not just a pretty face. Why are you doing this, Fletch?" she asked softly.

"I don't like thieves, I don't like seeing political prisoners who look like skeletons, I don't like knowing a place like the Abbey exists." His eyes met hers. "And I don't like to know that the men who killed your father and gave you six years of hell are living high on the hog in their little island paradise. I'm going to take it away from them and see that they burn in hell."

She gazed at him, stunned. "You're going to start a revolution over *me*?"

"No, I—" He stopped and nodded curtly. "Why not? I can't think of a better reason."

She laughed shakily. "I never imagined I'd ever be the kind of woman who would launch a thousand ships."

"I'd launch a million ships." He took a step closer, his hands grasping her shoulders, holding her gaze intently. "I'll get those bastards for you, Samantha. You don't have to go back there. Trust me." His words were soft, urgent. "They don't need you. This will be a different kind of war, fought mainly with power and economic clout. I know that battlefield better than you. Let me fight for you."

She gazed up at him, mesmerized by the force of his words and the hope they were building within her. "Why? Why is it so important to you?"

"Why?" he exploded, his hands tightening on her shoulders. "Why do you think? Because I'm scared silly you're going to go back there and starve in a cave. Because I'm terrified you're going to be captured or shot. Because I can't live without you now, you idiotic woman."

Joy like the nova of a giant sun flooded through her. It had come. It was here. Dear heaven, it was here!

"You mean it?" Her words were only a breath of a sound. "Fletch, do you really—" She stopped and suddenly tore away from him, her face lit with an inner radiance as she backed away from him. "Go out on the terrace."

"What?"

She turned and ran toward the stairs. "Wait for me on the terrace. I'll be right back."

"Where are you going? We've got to talk about this. There's no way I'm going to let you go back to St. Pierre with—" He broke off as she suddenly disappeared from view around the curve of the stairs. He was both exasperated and frustrated as he turned and strode across the foyer.

He was standing on the terrace looking out over the garden when he heard the French doors open behind him.

"I'm sorry to have kept you waiting; I tried to hurry."

He turned. "You pick the damnedest times to—" She was wearing the golden gown, and she was so beautiful that he forgot what he was going to say. Everything about her was radiant: the shimmering gown, her shining hair, her face. He cleared his throat. "You changed."

She nodded. "Everything but my shoes." She lifted the hem of her gown to reveal bare feet. "I couldn't find the matching sandals, and I was in such a hurry that I decided not to bother. I didn't think it would make any difference, anyway"—she released her skirt and came toward him—"since it's just the two of us. Now we can resume our conversation."

"May I ask why you're trying to vamp me?" He suddenly frowned. "You're not going to change my mind, you know. I'm not going to let you go back—"

"Hush." She stopped before him. "I'm not trying to vamp you." She grinned. "If I haven't done that by now, I'm in big trouble. And you know I wouldn't let you stop me if I really wanted to do something. I changed because I wanted everything to be absolutely right. I refuse to have another romantic moment spoiled because I feel like a grubby street urchin. The first night I wore this gown, I was walking on air and so full of hope that I was nearly dizzy. Everything went wrong then, but tonight it's going to be different."

"Is it?"

"Oh, yes." She took a step nearer. "Because you're going to tell me something

I've waited a long time to hear. You almost told me before I went upstairs, and now I want to hear the words."

"What do you want to hear?"

She shook her head. "Damn, you're a difficult man. All right, I'll go first. I love you, Fletch. I love your mind, your body, and that streak of idealism you won't even admit to yourself. I want to have your children and raise them, and then I want to spoil our grandchildren rotten. In spite of our agreement, I'm not going to leave you in two years, in twenty years, or in seventy years. You're stuck with me. If you ever try to divorce me, I'll probably murder you, and if you take a mistress, there's a good chance I'll murder *her*. Do we understand each other?"

He stared at her incredulously for a moment. Then he smiled with a joy so brilliant, it took her breath away. "Such violence," he murmured. "I believe Topaz has assumed control."

"You bet she has." She smiled up at him

lovingly. "And she's not going to let you off until she gets what she wants. *Tell* me."

"It's not easy for me," he said haltingly. "I've never..." He gazed down at her face. "God, I love you."

"Very good. How much?" she prompted.

"There aren't any words," he said simply. "You know what an inarticulate bastard I am."

"Try." Her fingers touched his cheek. "I won't ask you again, but tonight is special. Tonight it's important that I *know*."

"How can you help but know?" he asked gruffly. "From the first moment I set eyes on you I was practically torn apart." He turned his head so that his lips touched her palm. "I wanted to protect you and ravish you at the same time. You filled me with confusion and anger and..." He pressed her palm against his cheek. "Love. So much love that I thought it would kill me. For a while I believed I could control it, but that didn't last long. I was the one who was being controlled. And every day it gets worse because it gets better." He made a face. "Hell, just listen to me. I'm not even making sense."

"I think you're being very clear," she whispered. "That's the way I feel too."

"Then why didn't you tell me? I was worried as hell that you'd get bored and walk out on me."

She shook her head. "And I was being so careful not to make you feel boxed into a corner. You told me in the beginning how you felt about women interfering in your life."

"You should have known I didn't feel like that anymore. Didn't I spend every minute I could with you? Didn't I show you I couldn't—Stop laughing. This is a very serious point I'm making." Then he was laughing, too—free, joyous laughter. He grabbed her by the shoulders and shook her gently. "Okay, you're not a mind reader, and neither am I. We'll start over."

She shook her head. "No, we've already come a long way. We'll just continue on the same path." She stood on tiptoe to brush his lips with her own. "With love, Fletch."

His arms tightened around her, and he buried his face in her hair. "St. Pierre. You won't . . ."

"You could have asked me in the beginning instead of trying to stack the deck against my going back," she said soberly. "I've already fought my battles there. I'm glad there's a chance for St. Pierre to be saved, and I'll do everything I can to help make that come about." She felt him stiffen against her and added quickly, "With you, Fletch."

A sigh of relief shuddered through him. "Thank God." He lifted his head to look at her. "And thank you, Samantha."

"For what?"

"For loving me. Heaven only knows why you do. I'm so much older than you, and rough as hell, and God knows I'm nothing to look at."

She smiled up at him. "And I don't have your maturity, I'm independent as the devil, and will probably be so possessive that I'll drive you crazy. And you'll have to learn to live with Topaz as well as Samantha. So what? We'll still have it all, as long as we have each other."

He nodded slowly, gazing at her with glowing tenderness. "You're right." His voice was husky with emotion as he drew her closer with exquisite gentleness. "It doesn't make a damn bit of difference, love. We'll have it all . . . Topaz."